MW00814262

Riding Wood
A Sweet and Smutty Quickie

Abigail Graham

&

Vanessa Waltz

Copyright © 2017 Vanessa Waltz & Abigail Graham

All rights reserved.

ISBN:1542621917
ISBN-13:9781542621915

CONTENTS

ACKNOWLEDGMENTS

Thanks to Kevin McGrath for the cover design.

CHAPTER ONE

Alexa

I stand in a grove of redwoods that tower over me like silent soldiers. The trees are huge, so tall I have to stare straight up to see the highest branches. They swallow all sound. The stillness wraps around me. It heals the ache radiating at the front of my brain. Hours of listening to friends bickering about the cold will do that. The cloying scent of nature saturates the air. It's freezing, and my hands are stiff. I'm not dressed for the weather, but I need to be alone. Especially if I'm ever going to become the next Ansel Adams.

My frozen breath catches in my chest when I hear a rustle of leaves ahead. A deer head peeks around the trunk of a massive tree. Then the rest of her body follows. The doe picks through the brush, down to the gurgling water. She bends her neck to the ice-cold brook, and I carefully slide my Nikon out of the black nylon bag. Moving slowly, I pop the lens out and press the viewfinder against my eye.

So *beautiful*.

The doe's soft, brown hide comes into focus as I adjust the lens. Her delicate lips touch the water and my mouth stings as I imagine how cold it must be. A pink tongue darts out, lapping. Ripples disturb the gentle stream. My finger hovers over the button. I know that she'll probably bolt at the sound of the shutter, but I can't help myself. It'll be a gorgeous—

"DEER!" A lusty male voice breaks the perfect silence.

Her neck moves out of the frame.

Click.

The camera captures a blur of beige. I zoom out quickly even though she's already crashed through the brush. She's gone. Of course. And I'm going to kill the moron who ruined my beautiful shot.

"What the hell did you do that for?" I whirl around, locking eyes with a six-foot *boy*—I refuse to call him a man—dressed in a puffy black jacket.

Bryan.

This asshole hasn't left my side this entire trip, which I have Jessie to blame for. She thinks Bryan's the one who'll take my v-card. Last week it was Eddie. The week before that? She tried to set me up with Frank. The guy in Spanish class. I don't know why she's so *obsessed* with getting me laid.

Bryan lets out an impish laugh, still staring after the deer. "Were you taking a picture?"

"I was. Then you ruined it." *Dumb ass*, I want to add.

His smile falters as I storm past him, stuffing the

camera back into my bag. "Alexa, wait up!"

Oh fuck off.

It's not that I loathe men. I'm allergic to guys my own age. Their prodding fingers and sloppy kisses. Their inability to perform basic hygiene. A handful of disappointing sexual experiences was enough to know that I'm not interested in boys. They're just—*stupid.* There's no other word for it. The thought of handing over my virginity to a guy as dumb as a box of rocks makes my vagina want to shrivel up.

His broad hand slides over my shoulder. It's hairless and smooth, just like his face, which is slightly rounded with baby fat. Even his teeth look baby-like. They're so white and small. Maybe I'm brain damaged. He's the type of guy the girls in my art classes would probably brag about fucking, but I cringe at the sound of his voice. He *feels* all wrong.

I step away from his touch. "What do you *want?*"

He blinks at my hostility, confused. "Shit, 'Lexa. I was just—"

"Annoying the hell out of me." It's not like me to bitch out like this, but it's been three days of rebuffing his clumsy, not-so-subtle advances. I'm tired of it. "The whole point of this trip was to get away from campus. Lose

5

ourselves in nature. Take some photos. Not wreck every moment of peace and quiet!"

"I'm just trying to keep you company."

The idiot doesn't get it. "I don't want to be followed, damn it."

A smarmy grin crawls across his face. "Jessie said you'd play hard to get."

Oh God.

Let me guess. Jessie filled his head with nonsense about how I need a man in my life. "She says a lot of things."

He utters in a stage whisper, "She said you're a virgin."

A horrified shock runs through me. That *bitch* told him? Who else did she tell?

Bryan smiles reassuringly. "Don't be embarrassed. It's totally fine."

It's *fine.* He says it as though my virginity is a handicap. I might vomit. "Bryan. Go back to camp."

He turns and then hesitates. "Are you coming with me?"

My God, he's dense. "No. I'm staying behind."

"But it's kinda getting dark."

I don't care. "I'll be back soon."

"I don't think I should—"

"Go away!"

Without waiting for a response, I spin around and head

deeper into the forest. Rage ramps up in my chest, almost as strong as the frustration that's been building up for months. Despite my attitude toward guys, I've dreamt of the man of my dreams. Bryan sure as hell isn't him.

Unlike my friends, I know what I want to do with my life: pursue a career in photography. They're too busy getting shit-faced at parties, smoking weed, and riding cocks like they're on a carousel. It's not that I'm a prude. I've lusted after plenty of guys. Most of them unattainable or not interested.

Unfortunately I seem to be a magnet for the boys at school. Jessie says it's the way I dress. I look down at myself now, at the thin gray cotton stretched across my boobs, the V-neck showing off my cleavage. My face goes warm. I didn't plan on giving Bryan an eyeful, but somewhere along the hike I got hot and tied my jacket around my waist. No matter what I do or how hard I try, I always seem to attract guys I have zero interest in.

It's not fair. I just want my first time to be with a real man. Someone who knows what he's doing. A man who has enough self-control to last long, and who won't make me feel like I was made to please him.

A splitting sound makes me stop in my tracks. Heart beating wildly, I look around.

Crack.

The noise rips the air. Then I notice a sign up ahead: *NO TRESPASSING. PRIVATE PROPERTY.* Curious, I place a hand on a thick redwood and peer around the trunk.

There's a log cabin sitting just behind a thicket of branches and leaves. I admire the craftsmanship for a second before my gaze jumps toward the source of the rhythmic cracks.

My gasp hits the back of my throat when I see him.

A man—towering over six feet—wears a flannel shirt that's unbuttoned, revealing slabs and slabs of hard muscle and a sprinkling of dark hair scattered over his powerful chest. He wears a frayed pair of Levi's and scuffed construction boots. He grabs a log sitting on the ground, hefts the axe skyward, and then brings it down effortlessly.

I jump at the violent sound as the two pieces fall off the stump, perfectly split in the middle. He grabs the pieces—his hands are slightly dirty—and he throws them onto a stack leaning against the side of his cabin.

My jaw drops as he turns around, revealing a handsome face and scowling, dark eyes. For a second I'm paralyzed. Does he see me?

Then his gaze passes over where I'm hiding and flicks away. Pausing for a moment, he rolls the sleeves of his flannel shirt up his muscular forearms.

I can't stop staring at him. His jaw is covered with black stubble, and I imagine for a moment what it'd feel like against my cheek. Rough, no doubt, just like those hands gripping that axe. He holds it with a casual confidence, as though it's a part of his arm. I've never seen a man move like that, own the space he's in so completely. He looks like the sort of man who'd drink me in slowly. Even though he barely looked in my direction, I felt the intensity blazing through his eyes with a clench in my chest, which is so hot I feel like fanning my neck.

God, he's like a forest fire, radiating waves of warmth ten feet away. What would it be like to stand next to him? A blaze heats up my skin. I've never felt like this—at least, never from just *looking* at someone. My hand flies to my burning throat and my fingers graze my lips. I imagine it's him, touching me.

Licking my lips, I glance around, hoping I can sneak closer to get a better look at him or even take a picture.

Are you crazy, Alexa? That's creepy as hell!

I know damn well it crosses all sorts of lines to take a picture of a half-naked man on his private property, ignoring a sign that says to keep out, no less. But I can't help but want a better look at him. I'm a moth, helpless

9

against his flame.

I inch closer, quietly unzipping my bag and sliding my camera out as my heartbeat throbs in my throat. It nearly slips out of my grip. Then I aim it at him and pop off the lens, swearing under my breath as I zoom in to his chest. It's beaded with a fine mist of sweat.

Like a complete perv, I ogle this poor, unsuspecting man. His face blows up. I study every line, weathered by working hard outdoors. I slip down the gorgeous hollow of his cheeks to his strong jaw, the dip just below it, the Adam's apple just begging to be licked. Then I find his hands, searching for a wedding ring.

I nearly gasp. *Nothing.* How the hell is this man not married?

Swallowing hard, I zoom out to get Sexy Man in the Woods in my lens. He might not be married, but he's definitely not single. I don't understand how he'd survive a walk through town without a million women trying to jump his bones. For a second I consider going out there. Introducing myself like a normal person instead of creeping on him like a pervert.

The thought fills my stomach with lead. A man like him? No way he'd be interested me. I'll take my photo, print it, and set it on my desk. And I'll pine and my heart will ache every time I look at it. But it'll be worth it.

Even if it's totally inappropriate.

My hands shake. I take a deep breath as he swings the axe, admiring the way his muscles ripple. He pauses. Now's my chance. I wind back the camera, blood rushing in my veins. My finger trembles over the button.

Click.

The snap of the shutter carries through the forest, right into perfect hearing distance of Sexy Man in the Woods, who stops at once.

"Who's there?" he shouts in a gruff voice.

You idiot, you idiot, you idiot. I clap my hands over my mouth.

He buries his axe in the stump, searching the woods. A pair of dark, brooding eyes find me and hold me there. He sees me.

"Hi," I whisper, my breath coming out in a white cloud.

CHAPTER TWO

Lucas

The crack of the axe meeting wood splits the air and the two halves of the log, neatly divided, tumble to either side. There's a good-sized pile to either side of the heavy block where I've been growing my woodpile. The autumn days are warm enough once you get used to it out here, but the nights are getting colder, and I'll need a fire.

More than that, I need the work. A repetitive task to occupy my mind. Saw down the log with the chain saw, run the splitter, take the halves, the axe, and split them again. The shock of impact races up my arm. I feel the axe-head bite clean through and sink into the block. I lose myself for a brief moment.

I've been out on my homestead for six months now. I go days without talking to anyone. After I walked into my studio and found my now ex-wife riding her business partner, I decided I'd had enough of society. So I came out here to be with my first, truest love: oil painting.

I've got fifteen canvases of different sizes back in the cabin, all stretched over frames, all ready to become something. Michelangelo said he didn't create sculptures, he just carved away the marble to reveal the beauty beneath. Painting is the same. I dip my brush in color. Use it to peel away the blank canvas to unveil the truth underneath.

I used to, anyway. I haven't painted anything since I arrived here, haven't even picked up my charcoals and sketched. Every time I grab a palette or taste the heavy scent of oil paint, I hear the creak of my shoes on the wood of a converted mill loft. The soft moan Shelly made when she took Leonard, co-owner of the gallery I've been working with exclusively for years, echoes in my head.

I try looking into the canvas to find the truth, but all I see is the stark, crystal-clear image of Leonard's hairy balls pressed up against Shelly's cottage-cheese ass.

Shelly was my wife. I loved her. It didn't matter to me that she aged. I adored her flaws, the little marks around her eyes. She was the apple of my eye until I saw her fucking another man. Then she became something else entirely: puffy, saggy, and vaguely alien. I drive the axe-head home again and split the wood, as if I can cut away the grief I feel for the life I thought I'd built. I lived in a paper house.

Then I hear a soft click.

"Who's there?" I shout, my own voice unfamiliar and

raw from disuse.

My cabin is built in a narrow gully between two hills. A stream curves through it with the ease and confidence my brush once possessed as it transformed raw hue into meaning. Once in a while I'll see a deer; a doe ran through not fifteen minutes ago, bolting like something scared her. There are coyotes here, bobcats, the occasional bear. Between keeping my food in a larder on stilts, the scent of fire, and human habitation, I am left alone by animals. Other humans have the good sense to stay in civilization where they belong.

Until this girl. If you ran down a checklist of everything I'd fall for, she'd be eleven out of ten. She's maybe five-six, owing some to her brand-new, out-of-the-box hiking boots. She's underdressed for the weather that came through an hour ago. She took off her jacket and tied it around her middle, and her V-neck T-shirt displays the most wonderful cleavage. Her legs are bare in too-short shorts, which show off her long, smooth legs, kissed by a light, olive tan. Long, dark hair streaked with too-bright red frames a face that is at once sultry, womanly, and youthful, still soft from innocence.

I should tell her to fuck off from my land, but my cock is as hard as the axe handle in my hands.

"Hi," she whispers, though I see it more than hear it, a

brief pursing of her soft lips, untouched by makeup.

"Did you just take my picture?" I demand.

Her voice is high and clear, changing everything it touches. My serene little valley hums with activity.

"I was taking a photo of your cabin." She lifts her expensive camera as if to offer an excuse.

The cabin I was in front of. She was taking my picture. Splitting wood is sweaty work. I got hot and opened my shirt. I can feel her eyes on my chest, my stomach, like an invisible finger tracing down.

I leave the axe in the block and take a few steps toward her.

She takes a halting step back, clutching her camera in front of her like a shield, and puts her foot wrong. Her heel scuffs some wet leaves, and she goes down with a yelp. The girl slides down the gentle slope, coming to a stop right at my feet.

Still grasping her camera, she looks up, blinking her big, pretty eyes. I study her look of wonder mixed with embarrassment, fear, and something else. No woman has gazed at me like that in a while. Especially not lying on the ground before me. It wakes something up.

I reach down and take the heavy black thing out of her hands. She resists for a moment and then lets go. I think she expects me to glance at the picture she took, or maybe

15

smash it in a fury.

Instead I reach down, take her wrist, and draw her to her feet. She stumbles and bumps into me. For a half second I feel the soft weight of her breasts against my chest, and her scent floods my lungs. She washes in cheap soap, but it smells rich because it's her. All her money went into this camera.

"Are you all right?"

"I think?" she says, distracted. Her eyes haven't left me since she stood up.

I wish I'd shaved this morning. My once daily ritual has become biweekly unless I'm not in the mood. I've started to embrace it. Women shear off their hair after a bad breakup. Men grow beards.

The girl touches her own chin as if thinking about stroking mine. She leaves behind a streak of grime and flinches, glancing down at her hand.

"Damn, I'm filthy."

I would disagree. She makes the dirt clean, even the mud in her long locks. "Try a ponytail next time. What's your name?"

"Alexa."

"You're trespassing, Alexa. Can't you read?"

I don't know why I'm so gruff with her. Something about her awakens a primal feeling in my chest like the first embers rising from a newly kindled fire. Her legs are amazing, and up close I can see a full chest, hard stomach, and just a hint of bulk in her shoulders. She thinks she's a tomboy and doesn't realize that her fumbling attempts to dissuade men by hiding her lovely body just make her more enticing.

Her pretty face is a storm of emotions. There's enough of a girl in her that she wants to cringe because she angered an authority figure, an older man.

She starts to shiver.

Like I said, warm in the day but it'll be near freezing tonight. Night comes fast out here. The sun is already well below the tree line. The shadows are long, and the light, my God, the light loves this girl. She's a nymph, a princess slopped with mud. Like Cinderella.

She hugs herself.

"How far is it to your camp?"

She glances back and forth. "I don't know. I wasn't really paying attention. I'm not a hundred percent sure where I am, really."

The words tumble out of her like a confession.

"I'm Lucas. Come on inside, before you freeze. We'll get you cleaned up."

"Can I have my camera back?"

I hand it over, and she takes a look at her muddy hands

17

and changes her mind, hanging them by her sides before wringing her fingers like she doesn't know what to do with them.

The cabin isn't large, but it gets the job done. There's a small living room that doubles as my studio. I keep the blank canvases lined up against each other there, like patients in a waiting room. This place was meant for solitude, so there's one piece of furniture, a big plush sofa I bought secondhand and dragged down here by myself, facing the hearth the entire cabin is built around. There are two bedrooms in back. When I first laid out the plans for this place, I foolishly hoped I'd need a bedroom for my child. Or children.

As she steps inside, she droops her shoulders and looks down. She didn't mind walking near a *NO TRESSPASSING* sign or photographing me without permission, but she's ashamed to track mud into my home.

The way she tenses makes her ass a work of art in itself, a thing of beauty. She has a perfect, tight bubble butt begging to be grabbed, squeezed, and played with. I feel a hint of shame, wondering what noises she'd make if I bent her over the kitchen counter, buried my face in that ass, and tasted her pussy. I'd do anything to feel her legs quivering in my hands. The thought of her moans building as she loses control makes me so hard I can't stand it and I almost have to shove her inside to get my eyes off her perfect ass.

"Go on then," I grunt.

She steps inside and conscientiously stoops to unlace and then slip out of her boots. The simple pleasure of watching a woman in my home doing something innocuous, ignorant of how precious she is, is something I'd forgotten. I feel shame for how much I want to ravish her. I can already picture her tight body under mine, her long legs locked around me. I can't decide if she has tan lines. If her nipples are darker than her skin, bright pink, or blend in. The thought of her perfect round ass having a pale wedge from tanning in demure bikini bottoms makes my cock throb.

She looks at me with complete innocence. "I'm sorry to impose on you like this."

"There's a shower. We'll get you cleaned up."

She nods and finds the bathroom—it's not exactly a search. The cabin feels smaller now than ever when it's filled with her presence. When she takes a towel and disappears behind the cedar door, it's as though cold water splashes over my shoulders. My cock begs me for release, sings an image into my head of what her curvaceous body must look like.

Instead of my dick, I take charcoal in my hand as the

kindling licks flame into the logs piled in the hearth. I start to sketch. As much as I dream of full breasts, there is nothing in the world that feels as good as a woman's ass under my hands. I begin with her eyes and full lips, working outward to capture that first moment I saw her. My charcoal weaves in details that weren't there, like leaves and vines in her hair. They don't feel like additions. They feel like truth.

"Hey." Her voice cuts through the air.

I glance up to see her poking her head and one shoulder out of the bathroom, gripping the doorframe with one delicate hand. There's just enough of her showing to get a hint of how full her breasts must be.

"Thanks for the shower."

A sweet smile flashes across her face, and then she turns around. The towel shifts slightly to give me a brief view of her ass. Oops.

And yes, she has tan lines.

CHAPTER THREE

Alexa

As soon as the bathroom door shuts again, I lay my back across it and release a tense breath. *We'll get you cleaned up,* he said. As though he was going to march into the shower and soap up my body himself. I could have *sworn* there was a tone in his voice that hinted at more, but he stopped just short of the living room. I expected him to follow me. I wanted him to.

He's just being polite, you horndog.

Disappointment settles in my stomach as I strip the clothes from my body. There's no way he feels anything toward me but indifference, maybe a slight impatience to send me on my way. I should really wash up and get out of his hair before it's too dark, but I've never been in a man's bathroom before. So I do what any self-respecting girl would do the moment she's alone.

I snoop.

My slightly pale face stares back at me as I look into the mirror of his medicine cabinet. It's one of those mirrors that's covered with fog and chipped all along the edges. I swing open the door even as a voice tells me what I'm doing is wrong. My fingers graze over a short black comb. A razor. There's a stick of deodorant sitting on one of the shelves. I grab it and uncap the top, sniffing the bright-red gel. A shudder runs through me as the scent enters my nose, all aquatic and male. The same smell that wrapped around me when he touched me at the small of my back. I snap of the lid back on the deodorant and then I face the glass shower. There's a slightly damp towel hanging on the rack. A towel that wrapped around his naked, damp body this morning. I imagine it clinging to his waist, his chest beaded with moisture, his face rosy with the heat, just like I imagine it would be after sex.

Stop fantasizing about him. He's not interested, and he wants you out of his house.

But how can I stop when I'm in his home, naked and surrounded by the smell of him? My skin tingles as I walk through the cool air, which feels shared somehow. As if he's in here with me. I know he's sitting on the blue couch in his living room, probably counting the seconds until he can boot my ass out the door. I can't help but feel his voice run through me in a pleasant shiver, over and over again: *We'll get you cleaned up.*

Get a grip, Alexa.

The shower hisses loudly as I turn the knobs, filling up the tiny bathroom with steam. I let it wrap around, imagining him stripping off that flannel shirt to join me inside. What a sight that'd be. I saw little of Sexy Man in the Woods, but I could imagine what the rest of him looked like by studying the fit of his jeans and the mouthwatering bulge between his legs that promised a big, fat *cock*.

I stop in the midst of soaping my body, horrified at my thoughts. When you're a virgin at twenty-three, the first and last thought of your every waking moment is sex. Instead of wondering what it would feel like, my mind fills in the blanks as though it has already decided. What would *he* feel like? Would *he* even fit inside me? Would Lucas be sweet and gentle, or would he be as rough as his voice suggests? It runs through me again: *We'll get you cleaned up.*

My hand drifts lower, to where my body aches for attention. I slip down to my thighs, imagining the fingers are Lucas'. My gasp hits the ceiling when I touch my clit, already slicked with desire. I can almost feel his strong arm wrapped around my waist, pinning me against his hard chest as his beard scratches my cheek. He gropes my thigh and whispers with a harsh hiss that I'm his now, and he's not letting me go now that I wandered on his property.

An even deeper moan rips from my chest as I push my fingers inside. They pulse in and out, feeding that rich need to be filled that somehow never gets satiated. The blood pounds in my head, and I think how wrong it is to be touching myself like this. My eyes fly open and I stop, fingers still buried deep.

God. What would Lucas think if he knew I was in here, fantasizing about his body like some kind of sick pervert? He's a person. A man who already has someone. Well, I didn't see any photos of another woman. Hope warms my chest.

Bang, bang, bang.

My cheeks flush as he pounds the door. Oh shit. Did he hear me moan? Maybe he thinks I'm in trouble.

"Open the hell up," he says from behind the door. "*Now.*"

Whoa.

I shut the water off and stand there, trembling as I wring my hair out. "What is it?"

"Get your ass out here right now."

Heart pounding, I reach around for the damp, used towel instead of the fresh soft ones sitting to my right over the laundry hamper. He probably just wants me out of here, that's all. I took way too much time in his shower. I figure I have a reprimand waiting for me the moment I step out of the bathroom. That's what I'm expecting, but when I open the door he's right behind it. Holding my camera.

A violent blush rises to my cheeks as he stabs at the screen, which blazes with a photo of Lucas chopping wood. It's the most sexualized image of a man I've ever seen. Everything about it is perfect: the way his shirt reveals just enough chest, his brooding, sexy expression, the muscle rippling through his arms to tell you this man is *jacked.*

"What the hell is this?" he prompts, forcing me to look at the real thing.

I get lost in those intense eyes. "They're just photos."

A guilty feeling starts to worm its way into my stomach as he flips through the succession of shots.

His dark gaze cuts at me. "Explain."

It's hard to think in his presence, even more difficult when he takes that gruff tone with me that bodes no nonsense. I stare from my Nikon to his face, which is taut with suspicion. "I—you snooped through my camera?"

"Don't turn this around on me, sweetheart."

Sweetheart? A ripple of pleasure runs through me, even though he looks so forbidding.

"I found *you* trespassing on my property. There's a reason why that sign is up there: to keep people the hell out."

I tighten the towel around my neck. "I'm sorry."

The apology doesn't appease him. "Are you a journalist? Spit it out. The longer you wait to tell me, the worse you make things for yourself."

"I'm an art student," I stammer, blood rushing to my cheeks again. "Swear to God. Check my bag if you don't believe me. My student ID is in there. I was just taking photos because there's a contest in one of my classes. Whoever wins gets a spot at an art gallery downtown. It's a once-in-a-lifetime opportunity."

His smile is laced with darkness. "So you decided to find me, take pictures of me, and totally invade my damn privacy."

"What? No, I had no idea someone lived this far in the woods. Honest, I just wanted to get away from the friends I camped with. I guess I got lost and found your place, but I have no idea who you are." *Should I know him?* "Can I get dressed now?"

Lucas looks taken aback at being asked such a question and seems to remember that I'm standing in nothing but a towel, the water making plinking sounds as the drops hit the floor.

His gaze sweeps over my breasts, which are pushed up by my crossed arms. He looks at me for one long, hard moment. "Stay here."

I might fall to my knees if he uses that voice against me one more time.

He glances behind his back as he retrieves my bag, as though he can't trust me to be alone for one second.

Zipping it open, he finds the student ID and flips it in his long fingers. "Alexa Monroe," he reads. "I think you're a liar."

"I'm not lying!"

He walks toward me, slowly. "Put your damn clothes on."

I don't think Lucas wants my body covered, not when he holds my ID with enough tension to snap a piece of wood in two. "Is your wife coming home soon?"

"No wife." Pain shines through his eyes. "No girlfriend, either. It's just me here, which I'm sure will be great fodder for your article. Get dressed so I can walk you back."

I'm no psychologist, but a man building four walls to hide himself in seclusion like this is a man in pain. The towel slides down my arms slightly and Lucas watches as I tug it back up. Then he walks toward the couch, sitting down with a heavy sigh.

I retreat into the bathroom and fold the towel over the rack, wishing I knew who he was. He obviously thinks I know him from somewhere. Racking my brains, I try to think of who he might be.

Channing Tatum? Does he live out in the woods and surround himself with *NO TRESPASSING* signs?

Once I'm dressed I step out into the hall and gaze at

my surroundings. Beautiful oil paintings line the walls, all
initialed by the same artist: LW. There are more in the
living room: huge, charcoal figure drawings; watercolors,
portraits, and still lifes. There's an easel near his couch.
Lucas moves toward it protectively and covers the canvas.

My mouth gapes open as I find a small ink-wash
painting of a tree tucked in the corner. The wide brush
strokes are styled in sumi-e. I lean in close, studying it for
any flaws. There are none. A quick little scribble in the
lower right-hand corner tells me it's the same artist who
did the ones in the hall. LW. Could the L stand for Lucas?

"Wait, you made all these?" I turn around, whirling on
him. "Who are you?"

Lucas shoves his hands deep in his pockets, smirking.
"You really don't know who I am, huh?"

"No, but I wish I did so I didn't feel like such an idiot
right now. You have these beautiful watercolor and oil
paintings. The values, colors, and composition are just
amazing. And so many different styles." I can't quite
disguise the longing from my voice. "How do you do it?"

"Years and years of practice."

"But you're so young—at least—you *look* young. I
swear to God, I'm not a reporter or a journalist or
whatever you think I am. I'm just a photographer with
stupid dreams." When he frowns, I keep babbling. "I want

to be the next Ansel Adams."

He smiles. It tugs at me. "Ansel Adams didn't jump-start his career by taking photos of half-naked men." He stands and takes a giant step forward, invading my space.

Maybe he meant to push me back, but I don't want to move while his closeness burns my skin. I want to reach out and touch his face. There's something fiery in his eyes. Maybe it's what keeps him holed up in this cabin. Perhaps he's been alone too long. His gaze lingers on my lips, throat, and boobs.

I clear my throat. "What about Georgia O'Keeffe's paintings? Were they vaginas or flowers?"

"For six decades she denied there was anything sexual about her work. You don't get acclaim from the art world by drawing tits over and over."

My heartbeat throbs in my throat. "Says the man with figure drawings all over his walls."

"There's nothing new about nudity. Those are old and mostly for practice," he says flatly, gesturing toward the stack of blank canvases. "I haven't been able to make art in a long time."

"What about that?"

He sucks in breath as I point at the easel next to the couch, the one he was so keen to hide from me. "It's just a little sketch." He glances out at the sky, which is rapidly turning dark. "Look, I should take you back to your camp. I know these woods like the back of my hand, but we'd be stupid to walk in pitch black."

He doesn't fool me. I don't think he's any more willing to get rid of me than I'm willing to return to Bryan and that sellout, Jess. He looks at me through the eyes of a half-starved man.

Lucas doesn't know it yet, but I'm hungry, too.

How long have I waited?

I move around him and head toward the easel. I'm stopped by his hand grasping my wrist. "Don't," he says with the same authority when he told me, *Put your damn clothes on.*

"I want to see."

Reluctantly he lets me go and I walk behind it. I shift the paper hiding the drawing and gasp.

It's me.

A charcoal drawing of me, naked, with vines and leaves twisted in my hair. My eyes devour the details, wondering how the hell he imagined everything so perfectly.

"Wow."

Lucas clears his throat, looking neither embarrassed nor relieved. "It was just a fifteen-minute drawing."

Fifteen minutes. I couldn't accomplish this in hours. "Why me?"

He shrugs, and then an entirely different look falls on his face. "Why *not* you? I don't get a lot of visitors, Alexa. It's not like I can put out an ad for models to come to an abandoned cabin."

I stand in front of him, pulse racing for what I'm about to do. I unzip the hoodie and let it fall to the ground. Then I grab the hem of my shirt and slowly pull it over my body.

"Alexa, what are you doing?"

I ignore his tight voice and unbutton my shorts, letting them slide to the floor. "I'll be your model." He seems unable to speak as I reach around my back to unclasp my bra. "I want you to draw me. You need practice, right? It's the least I can do after ruining your night."

And I want you.

"There's just one thing you should know."

He grunts in the affirmative as my boobs bounce free. My beige, lacy bra hits the floor with a soft whisper. Then I hook my fingers in the edge of my matching panties, loving the way his gaze keeps stroking me. Up and down. Soft and hard.

"You should know that I'm a virgin."

CHAPTER FOUR

Lucas

My eyes follow her bra to the floor. Like most guys, my instinct when a girl exposes herself in front of me is to look away, but her lacy underthings draw my gaze like a flash of red before a bull.

Except that's bullshit. My eyes follow her discarded bra down so I can watch her underwear settle around her feet, then her calves as she steps out of them and nudges them to the side. I start at the bottom and take it to the top. Long, supple legs flow up to round, full hips, a flat stomach, full, perfect breasts, and a trembling, coquettish challenge in her eyes. She's biting her lip until the skin turns white and she doesn't even realize it.

"What the fuck are you doing?"

She puts her hands on her hips. The motion is hesitant, her entire being quivering with adolescent bravado. I can barely speak with all the blood rushing from my brain. She's fighting not to cover herself, wrap her arms around her chest, and squirm awkwardly to try to undo what she's done. Her nipples tighten into needy points, and I want them in my mouth as I thrust inside her.

"Oh, so you're fine with drawing my imaginary tits, but there's something wrong with the real thing? If you're going to draw me naked, you might as well represent me honestly."

The truth is, I didn't do her justice. She's gorgeous. Classical sculptors aspired for thousands of years to carve breasts as perfect as hers, and they all failed. Her flawless body astonishes me. I haven't felt this way in years, if ever. My cock throbs in my jeans, screaming at me to take her now. We stand locked in place for an awkward eternity, her display a challenge and an invitation. In my mind's eye, her belly swells, her breasts grow heavier.

"Are you going to let me pose, or not?"

I'm a virgin. The words ring in my head. Why did she say that? Just blurt it out like that? Was she trying to tell me that I'm privileged? She didn't need to explain that.

"Put your clothes on."

She ignores my order with a defiant smirk. "Where do you want me?"

"Out of my cabin."

"Naked?" she says. "I'll freeze."

When she says the word, I stumble over my own thoughts. My brain is starving, and my dick is close to taking control. She has a runner's youthful body, sweeping curves and languid lines. She is an artist's dream, the

33

perfect model. Her every movement is a symphony of light and shadow. The faint freckles on her shoulders and stark contrast of olive tan and creamy pale skin a challenge to my skill.

I want to paint her and I want to fuck her. "Clothes. *Now.*"

"You don't mean that."

The look on her face is opaque, her intentions lost by her clumsy attempts at seduction, pursed lips, and exaggerated stare. Her eyes plead far too loudly.

She's cute and precious and utterly fuckable. I can't stop thinking about how she would feel around my cock, the way her body would react to taking me. I have zero doubt that she's never been with a man before…even if she hadn't blurted out that she's a virgin.

She sits on the stool by the window and every tiny motion of her body is a struggle with the urge to conceal herself again. It only makes her more enticing.

"You want me to paint you?"

"Draw me like one of your French girls," she says.

I look her in the eye, because if I don't keep them on her face, I will stare at her tits. If I stare at her tits, I will put my hands on them. And if I put my hands on them, my tongue will follow, and then I'll have to taste her everywhere. It won't stop until we're tangled on the floor and I'm inside her.

She purses her lips and I imagine them wrapped around my cock, pressed hard as her cheeks hollow from sucking me down. I don't know whether I'd knot my hand in her hair and thrust, or caress her as she kneels between my legs.

"Are you supposed to stare at your subject like that?" She flinches slightly when I grab her arm. "What are you doing?"

The hint of fearful anticipation in her voice as the back part of her brain thinks, *Yes, this is actually happening,* tinges her voice beautifully. I soften my grip on her skin but turn her on the stool, positioning her arm and then her legs.

"Can you hold this pose?"

I should be ashamed. I have her posed to squeeze her magnificent breasts between her arms and arch her back. She shifts slightly on the stool and looks at me. I see it in her eyes, her sexuality awakening there like the first hint of a sunrise. This is perfect. She's perfect, and the sight of her wicked thoughts framed by her youthful face makes me want to explode.

"I think so," she says. "It's a little provocative, don't you think?"

Her foot brushes my leg as she shifts on the stool. I'm close enough to smell her. I taste the tang of my unflowery soap clinging to her skin, mingling with her light scent. Her hips touch my cock through my jeans and I shudder all over. It takes everything I have not to spin her around, throw her legs over my shoulders, and fuck her brains out.

Except I can't. She's not ready for that. The idea has never excited me before. I've never been with a virgin, never had any interest in it, but since she's told me, it's all I can think about.

"A little adjustment," I tell her. It's an excuse to touch her between her shoulder blades.

Her tits are so close. I think of the weight of them in my hands, the feeling of her lips pressed to mine. She looks hungry. Her body edges toward me without moving when I draw closer, our auras mingling.

I step back and the effort is like ripping my own arm off. Sitting on the sofa gives me the perfect excuse to cross one leg over the other to hide my raging erection. The sketch I started goes in the hearth, crumpled up so I can start over.

"You've posed before?" I ask as the image on the paper starts to take shape.

"With my clothes on." Her voice softens into a confession. "I've been asked to sit for nudes before but I never did it. This is the first time a man has seen me naked."

She swallows hard. I watch her throat bob, and her whole body shifts just slightly. The pencil stops moving in my hand as I focus on the subtle way her breasts move with her shallow breathing. I could paint every breath she takes and it would not be a wasted life.

"What's wrong?"

"Trying to capture some detail," I tell her, glancing down to continue the sketch.

"Why did you draw me with vines and stuff in my hair?"

I can't let her rattle me. I don't even know why I'm doing this…

Yes you do, you pervert.

It's an excuse to stare at her naked. Doesn't every artist dream of capturing a beautiful nude and then fucking the living daylights out of her?

"You keep licking your lips."

I posed her so her legs would block my view of the sweet treasure between them. If I can't see her soft lower lips, I can't imagine them swelling around my cock as I take her.

Focus, Lucas.

My chest is already aching. Once isn't going to be enough. She could be my favorite subject. I need to capture her as she was when she first stripped, her first fumbling steps into the raw power of a naked woman's sensuality. I also need to capture her growing into her confidence with every breath.

"Can I see it?"

"*No.*"

"Are you going to tease me?"

I can't help but smile. Her amateurish attempts at seduction take me back. I remember when I was so inexperienced that one little hint like that would make me cream my jeans.

She deserves that, a man who knows restraint.

"Don't move," I snap at her when she starts to shift.

"I'm freezing and my butt is going to have a permanent indentation from this stool."

I smirk. Her ass could crack walnuts. She has nothing to worry about, except my overwhelming desire to squeeze it. She is shivering, though, and not from nervousness at exposing herself. That's passed. I speed up my work; this won't be a finished piece, just the first of many.

I need to keep her here. I'll need a dozen studies of her in various poses before paint touches canvas. I have to do her justice.

Or is that just an excuse? The longer she's here, the more likely I am to break down and take her. That was her plan the moment she bared herself to me. There is some nagging doubt somewhere that it's all a ploy to exploit my connections.

She has talents, though. That pretty little head of hers is far from empty. I went through her photographs, all of them, and not just the ones of me. She has a natural gift for choosing and framing subjects.

Fuck, I'm so horny for this girl it hurts.

"That's enough for now. Get dressed and warm up."

Her inexperience shows. She squeezes her tits before she stands up, steps too hard so as to make herself jiggle. Then she bends at the hips with her long legs held taut as she scoops up her bra and panties from the floor.

God damn me to hell. I take a good look, and my mind floods with a dozen fantasies at once; her ass bouncing against my stomach as I fuck her from behind. Splaying her out on the bed, watching her wriggle as I finger her, the look in her eyes as I enter her. How warm and silky smooth she'd feel under my hands.

After she tugs her hoodie back on, she turns and looks at me. "So, am I a good model?"

"Maybe if you talked less." My tone is light, teasing.

"Ha ha." Then she shivers. "Can you put more wood on the fire?"

"Are you going to chop it for me?" I growl.

She makes a swing with an imaginary axe and thrusts out her flawless ass. I have to ball up my hands to stop from giving her a hard smack on that bubble. The burn on her skin and the look on her face would be worth it. She has a bratty streak, this one. Maybe something about me brings that out.

"First you trespass, then you use up all my hot water, and now you want to burn up all my wood. I figure you expect me to feed you, too."

Stupid testosterone-fueled urges to protect her flood my veins and harden my cock again. Once a woman has displayed her nude body, you can never look at her the same again. I look at her baggy top and know there's a goddess hiding underneath.

A goddess who isn't wearing a bra. She's still holding it. "You might as well feed me."

The only thing I want to feast on tonight is her, to feel her uncoil beneath me. The idea throbs in my head. Virgin, virgin, virgin. What if she's never come before? I picture her flushed and sweaty, her unfocused eyes full of reverence, desire, *worship.*

She sweeps around the kitchen island and stands next to me while I start up the stove. "What is that?"

"It runs on propane."

"Like the little ones at camp."

I give her an exasperated look.

She shrugs. "What are we having?"

I want to have you. Her eyes are so bright and innocent.

Damn it all to hell, I can't fucking stand it.

I lean in to kiss her. Alexa parts her lips. The warm sweetness of her breath is intoxicating, and the flood of sensation turns me all around. Her body molds to mine. My hand is in her hair, her legs around my waist, my fingers digging into her ass as my cock throbs against her stomach.

Still I don't kiss her.

I almost throw her onto the kitchen counter and fuck her right there, but I push her back. "We're having pork chops. Then I'm taking you back."

She blinks, confused. "But it's too dark."

I look at the window. She's right. Damn it. "You can sleep here tonight. There's a spare bedroom. And then you're going back where you came from first thing in the morning if I have to drag you."

She smiles, a big grin that melts something in my chest.

CHAPTER FIVE

Alexa

The cold sheets can't cool my burning body. All night I toss and turn, seized with a mad desire to tiptoe into Lucas' room and slip into bed with him. Sitting on that stool, naked, while a man I just met sketched me was the most erotic experience in my life. He barely touched me, but I felt every stroke of his pencil. Occasionally his eyes would flick up to study me. Though it wasn't warm in the living room, his burning gaze was enough to make my thighs slick. Lucas capturing my every detail while I sat there in the nude was so much more thrilling than the boys in college and their slobbering kisses. He drew me for over an hour, and when he was done his lips hovered a fraction of a centimeter away from mine.

He was really going to kiss me.

I closed my eyes and waited, heart pounding. I could almost taste his flaming heat, and then he pulled away. I told him I wanted to be his model, but I want much, much more than that.

Giving up on sleep, I throw back the covers and stand. I pick up the phone sitting on my nightstand. No new messages, even though I texted Jessica that wasn't coming home for the night and that I'd decided to bunk with a kind stranger I met in the woods. Her reply came at 2 a.m.: *K.*

Seriously, that's all I get? Never mind all the red flags, I'm supposed to be her best friend. Maybe I should've worded it differently, but I think there's a high probability she would've still sent me a *k.* Thanks for your concern, Jess.

Shaking my head, I pad through the cozy cabin in my bare feet and head toward the kitchen. It all comes down to priorities, I think. Girls my age are obsessed with having a good time. They're stuck in the present. Me? I'm all about the future. Husband. Career. Family. Preferably in that order.

Too bad the guys my age don't seem to give a damn about that. Not yet, anyway. Lucas on the other hand... He's so gorgeous and talented, I thought for sure he'd be married. But no girlfriend, either? That's crazy.

My tongue wets my lips. I enter the living room and pass the wonderful canvases. I pause near the easel. A shudder of pleasure runs through me when I remember him sitting behind it, watching me. It's insane that he's up here all alone.

Weak light filters into the cabin through the window.

Gray sunshine illuminates the neat kitchen, and I take a second to admire how tidy everything is. I crack open the fridge and find it well stocked with plenty of meat and vegetables.

What should I make him for breakfast?

A big guy like him probably eats his weight in protein every day. My eyes find a yellow carton of eggs and I grab it, smacking the door closed. Then I search his cupboards for a mixing bowl and find a clear glass one, cracking several eggs inside.

It's as though I'm made for this kitchen. The whisk is in the sliding drawer exactly where I thought it'd be, and it's not hard to find the rest of the ingredients. I don't stop to think if he would mind. Cooking makes me feel at home, no matter where I am. It's not a chore, especially if I'm doing it for someone I like. Photography is different. I have to think about the composition, the lighting, shutter speed, f-stop, *everything*. When I'm preparing a meal, my shoulders relax and my brain goes on autopilot. It's meditative.

For a moment I stand there and absorb the silence. I forgot what it was like to have a kitchen all to myself. Living in California doesn't exactly make it practical to rent a place on my own. The only way I could afford an apartment was to split it with Jess. I cringe, thinking of the cramped space back home. Jessica is nice enough, but the countertops are always cluttered with her empty Lean Cuisine boxes and rows of spices that she never uses. When her boyfriend comes over, I'm always the one who makes dinner. It's not an imposition, really. I look at it as saving them from boxes of overly salted, prepackaged crap.

I swipe my hand over the granite counters, admiring the steel hood and the wide sink. *This* is a fucking kitchen. Thinking of the pile of dishes waiting for me back home, I look around. My heart aches with envy. It's such a cozy place, and yet the kitchen's big enough that I don't feel cramped. There's a wide window in the living room that lets the dappled sunshine pour through. I imagine waking up here every morning, planting a kiss on my husband's rough cheek before making him breakfast like I always do. Then I'd fasten my hiking boots and step outside for a long walk, camera slung around my neck. How amazing would that be?

I'm still smiling at the idea when a voice booms from the living room. "What's this?"

Lucas stands in the hall, dressed in only a pair of dangerously low, hip-hugging sweats. The man is slabs and slabs of muscle, not an ounce of fat. He looks like he spends all day working his body to stay strong. From what

I saw yesterday, I don't doubt it for a second. He was chopping wood even though there was a stack leaning against his house. And I think if I hadn't interrupted him, he would've kept going. It was as though he was punishing himself.

"Are you going to answer me, or are you going to keep staring?"

The sight of him is enough to make my words stumble over each other. I feel like a foolish young girl as I sweep my arm over the stove. "Breakfast."

The tantalizing smell of bacon draws Lucas forward. There's a scowl on his face that I decide is extremely sexy.

"Don't worry," I add quickly. "I'll clean everything up. Promise."

But the frown doesn't vanish from his forehead and he doesn't back down. He stops a foot away from me, hanging back as though afraid to get too close to me. "I'm the one who's supposed to feed you."

Why the hell does that sound like sex? *It doesn't. Stop it.* "I-I don't mind cooking. I do it all the time for Jess and her boyfriend."

"Yeah, but you're my guest." He smiles. "Or trespasser. Whatever, it's my job to make sure you don't go hungry."

I wonder if he's the type of man who dotes on his woman. I'm getting that vibe, and it warms me to my toes.

"You could still feed me," I say in a coy voice.

His smile widens, dimples carving deep into his cheeks. "I bet you'd love that, wouldn't you?"

How badly do you want to fuck me after seeing me naked? I wish I had the balls to ask him. I wish I could read his mind. I wish he'd close the distance between us.

But he doesn't.

"I would."

Lucas breaks eye contact and clears his throat. He pushes off the kitchen counter, turning away from me to head straight toward the freshly brewed coffee. He pours two cups as I ladle eggs onto his plate with several strips of bacon. He grunts a thank-you as I hand him his breakfast, and then I shut the burners off and join him at the table. Everything is already set with knives and forks. I even found raspberry jam in the fridge and set it in the middle, along with a stack of toast.

He spears one of the pieces with his fork and gives me a look. "How did you know where everything was?"

I shrug. "Sixth sense, I guess. You're great at organizing."

He laughs. "You haven't seen the mess in my living room?"

"That's not a mess, that's an art studio. Believe me, I know how it is."

"Do you?" Still the note of suspicion.

"Of course. It must be great having a private place you can call your own."

"Not so private, as it turns out."

I blush, but he gives me a smile and wink that makes my stomach flip. Why the hell did he have to be so perfect?

"I built the cabin for that reason." He makes a face. "I had to get away from all the chaos in the city. All that noise. The adulation and the awards—all of it meant nothing the moment I couldn't put my charcoal to paper. Don't you ever get stumped?"

Shaking my head, I watch him as he cuts the egg in half with the edge of his fork. "My career has barely started. Calling it a career is probably generous at this point, but when you've seen so little of the world it's hard to get bored, you know?"

"You are so young. So innocent."

Then it's my turn to grin. "I'm not *that* young. Twenty-three isn't exactly jailbait."

"What we did last night…" He shakes his head. "I shouldn't have done it, Alexa. I apologize."

"For what? I loved modeling for you. Besides, it shouldn't matter how old I am if it's strictly professional."

"It's different with you," he says, eyes cutting at me.

"You're a beautiful young woman, and I've been alone too long."

Yes you have. "Then what are you waiting for?"

His nostrils flare at my suggestion. "We can't. I'm practically a mentor to you."

"I don't know who you are!"

"It doesn't matter. I shouldn't have taken advantage of you."

"I might be a virgin, but that doesn't mean I'm innocent." I stand from the chair and walk to his side as he remains seated, his fists clenched on the table. Christ, if he knew the dirty thoughts I had about him in the shower and how I touched myself in those sheets. "Do you even know why I've saved myself all these years?"

His mouth parts, eyes trained on me like a beast seconds from pouncing on its prey.

"I didn't know at the time, but I was looking for a man like you."

Warmth catches my wrist. I look down and see him lightly grasping my arm. An electrical shock runs up into my heart, which pounds so loudly I think he can hear it.

He stands. The chair groans. All I can think about is his hip, bumping into mine. His hand curving over my shoulder.

Kissmekissme.

His breath billows over my mouth. "I fucking want you."

Oh my God. I think his cock is digging into my thigh. It feels like a gun, so thick and hard. I look down, but he catches my chin and forces me to meet his gaze. "I want you, too."

"You want the man who impresses you. Who makes the art on these walls."

I snap my mouth shut because it's true, isn't it? "Please, Lucas."

"No." The quick word blows across my lips. "Let's get you home."

* * *

All the way back to town, I kick myself for how badly I screwed up with Lucas. After years of frustration I finally meet someone amazing and he won't kiss me. Won't even touch me. Maybe I'm not his type after all.

No, I refuse to believe that. Not when only minutes ago I felt his cock against my leg. I wished I looked at it, grabbed it through the thin fabric of his sweatpants. He almost kissed me—*again*. I can't take much more of this teasing.

Lucas is as cool as a cucumber. He drives his pickup with one hand, the other lying casually on his thigh. A swell of heartache builds inside me when I imagine linking my fingers through his, and his answering smile. I'm not going to be one of those girls who cries and acts pathetic when the man she wants turns her down.

Even when that man is only trying to do the right thing.

"Where did you say your friends were staying?"

As it turns out, Jessica and the others couldn't hack it in the cold. She texted me this morning before my battery died to tell me that they were bunking in a motel in town for the rest of the weekend, and I should join them there.

"At the Motel 6. Jess got two rooms, I think. I'll have to share one with Bryan, I guess." I cringe at the thought.

"Bryan?"

Is it wrong that his grating tone makes me happy? Well, it does. "Yeah, we're in the same photography class. He's harmless, but really not my type."

Lucas recoils. "Why the hell didn't she get you separate rooms?"

"Why do you care so much?"

He makes a sound that's halfway between a growl and a shout. "You shouldn't be sleeping in a motel room with a guy you have no feelings for. It's not right."

"Relax, I'm sure Jess will switch rooms around if I tell her I'm uncomfortable with it."

The tension slackens his shoulders, but his knuckles are

still white when he pulls into the parking lot of the motel. He gives it a grim look and then turns toward me. "So."

"Can I get your number?" I ask, keeping my voice innocent. "Just in case something happens."

He heaves a sigh as though I'm demanding something unreasonable, but he reaches in his back pocket and programs my number into his phone. I do the same when he rattles off his number. Then I almost grin because Lucas has no idea I have no intention of giving up on him that easily.

Feigning indifference, I shrug and reach for the doorknob. "Thanks for the hospitality, Lucas. It was wonderful meeting you."

"*Wait*," he says, and joy erupts in my chest. I expect him to start the car and drive away, to tell me he didn't mean it, that he doesn't want me to leave. It's all over his face.

"Be safe," he says.

Be safe?

My jaw drops as he shifts the pickup into reverse—my cue to leave. And I open the door, stumbling into the blinding sunshine. I hold my arm above my eyes, and he gives me a perfunctory wave as he pulls out of the parking lot.

Be safe.

That's what you tell a little girl before she walks to school. Where is the man who said he fucking wanted me? I feel like dust on the side of the road as he drives into the back toward the small, winding path that leads to his secluded cabin. Be safe. Fuck that.

I'm so angry I don't know where I'm marching off to, but apparently my brain has a mind of its own because I walk toward the nearest gas station. It's a small operation, and suddenly I see a man in overalls leaving a bathroom. The steel door slams shut. I rush forward and wrench it open. Squalor greets me as I step inside the damp bathroom. The rank smell of piss saturates the confined air and there's graffiti, violent whorls of black all over the doors. There's no toilet paper. The mirror behind me is cracked and dirty. It's no place for me to relieve myself, let alone get naked, but that's exactly what I do.

I undress. I let every stitch of clothing fall on my bag, which sits near my feet. Only when I'm naked and shivering do I take the cell phone from the pocket in my shorts. I swipe it open and search for Lucas' name, and then I open Messages.

God, I can't believe I'm doing this.

I take photo after photo of myself standing naked in this dirty bathroom, a thrill running through me every time one goes through. I imagine him alone, curled up on his

53

couch. His phone dings with an alert, and he lazily picks it up, not expecting to see me. I wonder if he'll touch himself, and just the thought of that makes my pussy clench. Reaching down, I slip a trembling hand between my thighs and part my petals. *Snap*. Another picture. My fingers slide inside. *Snap*.

My fingers won't stop. I can't. I've been riding a wave my whole life, waiting for it to come crashing down. It builds inside me as I wipe my wetness over my clit, rubbing hard. My cheeks blaze. All I have to do is think of him, standing next to me. *Lucas*. Touching me. Then the crescendo hits, and my pussy clenches hard around my fingers. A wave of pleasure shudders through me as I open a new text bubble and write: *For reference*.

CHAPTER SIX

Lucas

This is a mistake.

Leaving her behind is the right thing, and the right thing has never felt so completely wrong.

I've been in the woods too long. I'm having conversations with my pickup truck. Now that Alexa is gone, I have no one to talk to.

Not gone, though. I can see her in the rearview mirror, standing there on the sidewalk, watching me leave. As if to mock me, the wind picks up a little and brushes her hair away from her shoulders so it catches the late-morning sunlight.

Sketching her only once would be a waste. Every moment of her could be art.

I grunt and choke the steering wheel too hard for just a moment. The old vinyl creaks under my hands. Better to forget and move on. She's inspired me. I created something for the first time in God knows how long.

The ride back up the mountain always feels longer than the ride down. I make the trek every other month or so for supplies and to stop at the café to check my email and bank accounts before I return to the welcome seclusion of my own little world I've carved out in the earth. I visit the town but don't know it, and it doesn't know me.

The mountain does. Once I leave the paved road for a dirt one and then the dirt road for a trail, the concentration needed to avoid flipping the truck squeezes the rest from my mind. I always liked driving. Didn't get much of a chance when I lived in the city.

When I finally kill the engine and open the door to step out into the chill, the hot puff of mist in front of my lips is like the ghost of Alexa, so close. I shouldn't have let myself do that. I close my eyes and feel the warmth of her, the buzzing anticipation of her mouth a breath away from mine. The promise of a kiss twists like a knife in my chest.

It's silly. She wouldn't want what I want.

I throw the door closed and step away from the truck, hands thrust in my pockets. It's going to be a cold one today. I hope she has the sense to wear, well, pants, to start with.

This is what I mean. A girl her age wants the excitement of midnight trysts, fooling around with other people in the room, the irreplaceable joy of a first kiss, a first touch, a first...everything. I can't help but smile at the thought of Alexa's half-baked attempts at seduction, one moment all smoldering seduction and the next blurting out that she's a virgin. She probably thought that would rev my engine like I'm some inexperienced boy.

She wasn't wrong. The thought is like icing on the cake. I would be her first. She would be mine, totally, utterly, irrevocably. If I were a lesser man, I would take pride in knowing that she'd compare everyone after to me, and no fumbling amateur could compare to what I'd do for her, to her... But I'd never let her have another.

The idea, the image, keeps creeping back into my head. There is something past picturing her naked, although I can't keep myself from that either. I envision her on the couch. There's a kitten in her lap; I bought it for her, and her belly is big and round. My son is curled there, waiting to join the family. She's wearing a sweater she knit for herself and I have a matching one. It's hideous but I wear it anyway. The fire and the wool make me hot, but I wear it because she wants me to.

I top off my silly little dream with a decorated Christmas tree in the corner and the smell of pumpkin pie.

Family.

Sometimes you don't know how badly you need something until you realize you'll never reach it. I need her like a drowning man needs the safety of the shore. With water in your lungs, wet sand under your hands is paradise.

This cabin was my refuge, the shore I clung to when I

was drowning. Now the sand is cold where it should be warm, and it sucks me down and crushes my lungs.

It's empty. Fucking empty. I'm going to erase the evidence of her. I'm going to clean the dishes she dirtied, banish the smell of the bacon she fried, and it won't help. The ghost will still be here. I won't be able to see the counter without picturing her leaning against it, or the stool in my studio without thinking of her bare skin resting on it.

I close my eyes and shudder then go about my daily chores. I hew wood. I clean. I climb up to the larder and bring down tonight's meal.

I left my phone on the counter. I probably seemed old to her when she saw it. The phone is just a plain one that's barely capable of receiving pictures. I needed a lifeline just in case, but I didn't want any Internet or contact with the outside world.

Except her. She texted me.

I sigh. I should toss it in the fire and grab another one on my next trip to town. End it now, put her out of my head. Except I catch a glimpse of my sketch of the beautifully innocent wood nymph and open the damned phone anyway.

The newest text comes before the others: *For reference.*

What follows sucks all the blood out of my brain, along

with all the sense. A series of artfully composed nude selfies, and I don't mean that ironically. She knows how to use even the bad lighting of a dingy bathroom. Only her outstretched arm ruins the effect of the best one.

She put the light behind her so it haloes her head. The harsh glow of bare fluorescents becomes a corona, glowing in her soft, luscious hair. The subtle red streaks give her a playful air along with her lustful smirk.

Even in pictures like this, she knows composition intimately. She shows just enough skin, covering her breasts with her arm, to drive me wild. I feel like she's just learning what she doesn't show can be as alluring as what she does. A little modesty is as enticing as the bold display she gave me last night.

Before I realize it, I'm hard as a rock and unbuckling my belt. I fall back on the couch with the cell in my hand, all the lamps in the cabin unlit so there's nothing but the phone's light.

The images she sent are only the first steps. As I stroke my cock, my eyes go lidded and the phone drops out of my hand. I use everything at my disposal: the memory of my hand on her wrists, her tits brushing my chest, and the enticing scent of her hair. I think of her under me on a bed of clean grass, her body opening.

I see it. Feel it all. The smoothest skin of her stomach

caressing mine as she arches, gasping in shock and satisfaction as I fill her for the first time. I can't stop thinking about claiming Alexa, taking her, making her mine. I pump my hand faster, imagining her walls gripping me. Her eyes open wide as we kiss, begging me in a silent plea to fill her up and make a baby with her.

The thought of lying with her after the deed brings me over the edge. Her body presses against mine as I lie on top of her. I'm still inside her when I weave vines around her finger to make a ring. She glows as my seed takes root inside her.

My shuddering, wordless cry echoes in the empty cabin. I'm alone again and cold. I wash up and take a quick Navy shower with a burst of very, very cold water to slow the racing of my blood and shove Alexa out of my mind.

The logs clatter as I make a pile in the hearth. The flames give me good light to work by. I set up a canvas on the easel and start preparing my tools.

In minutes I'm painting so frantically I swear and strip off my shirt. My strokes are sure, quick, precise, like the canvas is covering the image and I'm slicing it away with bold cuts and scrapes.

I don't realize I'm painting her until she appears in the landscape I've created, a wild, fantastical exaggeration of the scenery around the cabin. There are rocks, a stream, tall trees, and flowers everywhere. It's an explosion of color. Even the small image of Alexa standing on the ridge commands everything around her, turns the splendor of the wild into a setting. She becomes the center of everything. I draw a wreath of flowers in her hair. The blossoms are so small they're just daubs of color and shadow. They curl around her toes.

I step back, breathless. I haven't worked so fast in years. The image just exploded into being on the canvas, passing through me as though I were a door to wherever it came from.

Gently I set it aside and start a new one. This composition is more intimate, focused on the way the stream eddies around a rock about a thousand yards before the cabin. I have no intention of painting Alexa into it.

Then she's there, taking shape in creamy porcelain before light and shadow build her into the center of the image again. She sits on the boulder facing away, the water sweeping around her dangling toes, as naked as the day she was born. Her long, silky hair drapes down her bare back as she turns to peek over her shoulder, a hint of the outer curve of her breast complementing the sweeping shape of her back and hips. I mean to make her pout, but she smiles instead. A knowing smile.

My hand is trembling. Am I ever going to paint anyone

or anything else again?

I resist the urge to smash both paintings and throw them into the fire.

They're good. They're the best I've done in years, maybe in my entire career. But they're not right. I can't capture her unless I can paint from life. I want to make her a goddess, immortal, perfect, and preserved on the canvas forever. A lasting statement of beauty.

I want that as much as I want her belly to swell with my child, to cook her breakfast, hold her and laugh at her jokes.

Two paintings in one day. They're sloppy and don't capture their subject. A third would drain me. I set them both aside, lean against the wall, and throw more wood on the fire to warm my little domain before I crawl into a cold bed that will never be warm enough.

How long will it take for this to fade? Will I have to burn down this cabin and build a new one to find a place where she doesn't haunt me?

I sleep and dream of Alexa. I wake with the taste of her on my tongue, the feel of her in my hands, the warmth of her on my skin, and the desire for her straining my cock. It throbs with need.

Work. I need to work.

I might as well capture this energy while I still have it.

My supplies are running low.

I need to visit the art store. It's a simple practicality. I have no ulterior motive.

So I mount up in the truck and twist the key too sharply, as if to vent my frustrations. It coughs in the cold in protest but sputters to life anyway, and I drive back down the mountain. I let the task of backwoods driving give me the focus I need not to think about her.

The art store is a local mom-and-pop shop, not that I care. It used to be the first floor of a sprawling house. The owner and proprietor, a round woman who looks like she used to teach schoolchildren, sits behind the front counter reading a cake decorating magazine and does not acknowledge me.

She does, however, glance at the source of the voices in the store, annoyance twisting her grandmotherly features.

"What are we doing here?" a girl's voice says.

"I can't believe we were *in* the woods," a boy says back. "It's freezing. What was the point of this again?"

I can even recognize Alexa's exasperated sigh.

She doesn't see me as I step to the end of the aisle. The store is cramped, the shelves reaching almost to the ceiling, cramped at their tops with dusty supplies and blocks of clay that have long ago turned to stone, unbought.

With Alexa's back turned to me, I see a boy lay his arm

across her shoulders. He has a look to him that reminds me of my old classmates from another life. He edges in closer, ignoring the way she stiffens, turns her head to the side, and denies him the kiss he's so desperate for.

"Baby, why don't we worry about the homework later. Let's head back to our room."

"We're switching rooms," Alexa says. "I'm not sleeping with you, Bryan. Get over yourself."

Liquid rage seethes in my veins. He has no right to touch her. A simple, animalistic instinct takes over and I storm toward him.

She's mine.

She shrugs out from under his arm and storms away, almost walking into me.

Alexa does the worst thing she possibly could—she gives me a genuine, warm, surprised smile, her face lighting up.

"You came back?"

I do the worst thing I possibly could.

I brush aside the strands of hair from her face and cup her cheek. Then I steal her breath with my kiss.

CHAPTER SEVEN

Alexa

This must be a dream. It's so rare that things actually work out that I expect to be yanked awake, my heart pitter-patting with the vestiges of his kiss. Except this wasn't how I imagined our first kiss: in the art store, my back pressed against the bags of printer paper, the fluorescent lightbulbs burning above me, and Bryan pouting a foot away.

But not even Bryan could ruin this.

I taste Lucas' breath before his lips. My mouth opens in surprise when he descends on me, crushing his lips against mine. Possessive hands curve around my arms, pinning me back against the shelves of glossy printer paper. His thigh slides between my legs and my core reacts violently, clenching hard on a space aching to be filled. His kiss stuns me. Knocks me off my feet.

He's kissing me.

I wrap my arms around his neck as his taste swirls in my mouth. I curl my fingers into his thick hair, inhaling a heady scent. Pine and sweat. It's like walking through a cloud of man when browsing the men's department at

Macy's. I hang on to his broad shoulders because every kiss makes my heart want to leap out of my chest. He's rough, all tongue and bite. I lean into him, and he pulls back only to dig his fingers deeper into my hair. A slight tug from his fist, and our lips break. I breathe deeply, skin tingling from the gusts billowing from his mouth. My mouth is raw from his unshaven jaw. He notices and smoothes my cheek.

God, that wasn't just a kiss. There's something tender in his gaze and in the way he holds me, even as his growing hardness digs into my thigh. I study every wrinkle that creases when he smiles, the rough stubble on his cheek, his slightly swollen lips.

"Uh," a grating voice interrupts us. "What the hell, man?"

Jesus, I forgot he was here.

I turn around and almost jump because Bryan is standing *way* too close. He scowls like a toddler denied a treat. He completely extinguishes the glow from kissing Lucas. What a fucking buzzkill.

He doesn't walk away, which is too much to ask of Bryan. Nah, I shouldn't expect him to behave like a fucking adult and not like Lucas pissed on his favorite toy.

I glare at him for several seconds. "Bryan, this is Lucas."

"Cool," Bryan forces out.

Why are you still standing here? "He let me stay in his cabin last night."

I figure that'll be the nail in the coffin, the kick in the ass he needs to go away, but of course I'm wrong.

"Oh," he says in that kind of voice. Comprehension dawns on his face, and then he has the balls to look pissed off. "Seriously? You gave it up to *this* guy?"

Wow. I open my mouth to tell him off, but Lucas gets there before me. "That is none of your damn business."

He snarls at Lucas. "No offense, but aren't you a little too old to be picking up college chicks?"

Lucas lets a growl slip into his voice. "If I were you I'd take my hurt feelings and fuck off."

"It's an honest question."

"And I'm twenty-nine." *Moron*, he doesn't add.

Now I'm getting annoyed. "Bryan, go away."

Wounded, he turns his attention back to me. "Geez, I'm just trying to help."

"You're interrupting," I snap.

But he doesn't get the hint. Instead he puffs out his chest even farther, looking like an emperor penguin. "Look, man, she's not, like, some piece of meat you can just grab whenever you want."

Lucas doesn't even look at him. He makes Bryan

67

stumble backward as he pushes him aside in the same manner a bear might swat at a cub. A giddy feeling rises in my chest as Lucas wraps his arm around my waist, leading me out of the store.

"Who the hell is that boy?"

Are you jealous? "Just a guy who was hoping to pop my cherry on this weekend trip. Seriously. He offered to while I was taking photos in the woods. That's kind of how I found you."

His grip tightens on my waist as we step into the bright sunshine. His fingers seem to burn right through every layer of clothing I'm wearing.

"Did you get my texts?"

"You know damn well I did." He squeezes me. "After I saw those pictures, I couldn't just let you bunk with some college kid who'd probably blow his load in the first five seconds."

"Does that mean you'll blow your load inside me?"

I bump into his chest when he suddenly stops. He cradles my head, his thumb brushing against my bottom lip. "If you don't stop talking filth and sending me dirty pictures, I might forget that you're a virgin and bend you over my goddamn car hood."

Do it.

My heart leaps when he guides me toward his pickup

truck, but he releases me to open the car door. Then he helps me inside. The door shuts, and my pulse pounds in my head for those few seconds that I'm alone.

Oh my God. He's taking me back to his secluded cabin in the woods. Does that mean he's going to fuck me? Please tell me that's what he wants.

The door opens before I can decide what to do about it. "What is this, Lucas?"

He slides into the seat, giving me a look full of heat. "I'm saving your ass from that loser. That's all."

"And whisking me away to your cabin to make sweet love to me?"

The sound of his hands grinding the steering wheel makes my stomach leap. "I didn't say that. You need a place to stay, and I'd feel like an asshole if I left you here."

"You sound like you're trying to convince yourself that's all it is."

The car roars to life as he turns the ignition. His eyes cut at me. "Don't start, Alexa. You don't know a damn thing about me."

"I know you saw my photos and came rushing down here like a bat out of hell. You kissed me."

"Yes, I've been alone for too long and *yes*, I won't deny being around a girl like you is tempting as hell, but I'm not a caveman."

Lucas is dead wrong about that. He practically yanked me out of Bryan's greedy hands and forced his tongue down my throat in the middle of the local art supply store. Us women notice these things.

"So you're my knight in shining armor, huh?" My back sinks into the leather as he pulls out of the parking lot.

"Not exactly, sweetheart."

* * *

Sitting here is an exercise in patience. Flames lick up my back as I sit on the stool, surrounded by the warmth of a crackling fire. My clothes lie in a pile on the floor. This time his greedy eyes didn't look away when my panties hit the ground.

This time I'll have him.

The tight four walls of Lucas' cabin close in on us, so small that there's no escaping this heat. He rolls his sleeves to his elbows as though I'm the fire, and being close to me is too much.

I thought being a figure model would be a nerve-wracking experience, but it's not with Lucas. Being sketched by an artist like him, the only man who's ever seen me naked, and the only man I've ever felt a soul-deep connection with, makes it an intensely erotic experience. I watch his eyes follow the curve of my breasts, and his hand follows with a sweeping motion. He never meets my gaze. So precise. Dedicated.

I can't sit here much longer. My mind keeps teasing me with images of me climbing onto his lap to straddle his waist. I want his fist in my hair.

"Thanks for doing this, Alexa" he says, his voice cracking the silence. "You're an amazing subject."

I hope I can be an amazing fuck, too.

If I'm being honest with myself, that's what I'm really worried about. But I don't know if I'll ever figure it out, because he keeps behaving all professional when more than an hour ago he told me he wanted to bend me over his hood and *fuck* me.

And the thought makes me want to touch myself.

Why don't you?

My lips curve.

Yes. Let's see how well-accomplished artist Lucas Wood controls himself when I have my fingers deep inside my pussy. I'm coy, at first. I spread my legs, giving him a full view of my innocent pussy.

The sound of the scratching pencil halts as I lower my right hand to my mound, parting the delicate petals aside. I touch myself with two fingers, sliding in the thick juice. He watches me, not even pretending to draw anymore. Instead his gaze is irresistibly drawn to the ache between my legs.

"Alexa—"

But his voice cuts off abruptly with my gasp when I penetrate myself, making my fingers curve upward to hit that sweet spot. I'm so wet it's obscene, full of fire for the way he looks at me right now, his eyes locked on my pumping fingers. My lips feel hot. I touch my boobs with my other hand. Grab the nipple and squeeze.

"Alexa," he says in a stronger voice. "That's enough."

"Or what?"

I insert a third finger, widening my pussy just enough to make it hurt. He slams the pencil on the easel and gets to his feet. His long, thick cock is raised against his jeans, the fabric stretched so much it looks painful. It would be incredibly sexy if it weren't for the fury thickening his features.

"I want you. You want me. What are you waiting for?"

He beats his anger down. Tries to look away. He can't.

I clench over my fingers, the wave of pleasure rising with every thrust. No, I don't want to come yet. My chest heaves as I slide my fingers out, and then I'm seized by a filthy thought. One that I know will drive Lucas to the edge.

I bring my wet fingers drenched in my pussy juice to my face. And I open my mouth to suck them clean. My lips barely touch them.

He makes an animalistic sound before grabbing my

wrists. The stool topples to the floor, but his arm wraps around my waist. He lifts me. I knew he was strong, but even I'm surprised by how easily he hoists me into the air. Then my mind is preoccupied with one thought: he's holding me.

I've never been held like this. His arms wrap around me gently; even though his hold is firm, his guidance is sure. He takes me—not to the bedroom—but to the kitchen counter. Good, it's closer. And he sets me down so that my legs hang off the edge.

Lucas' angry breath hits my lips. "You're a dirty girl, Alexa."

"I know. I'm sorry."

"No, you're not." His arm is still wrapped around my back. "But I know I'll be after I do this."

What?

Suddenly he stoops down, his face close to my body. Oh my God. His beard tickles me on the way down. Then he roughly seizes my knees and forces them apart, opening the very essence of my ache for him. His hot breath billows over my wetness and my core clenches hard.

"I'm going to eat your pussy, Alexa, because I can't take it anymore."

There's a hitch in my chest. *Eat your pussy.* I'll never forget the way he said that.

He leans in, his dark head between my legs, way closer than any man has ever been. His lips press against my throbbing pussy. I feel the seal like a hot poker. My pleasure dials to ten as he reaches back with his long tongue and licks, all the way back. Then he does it again.

"Oh my God!"

When his slick heat reaches my clit, he does a swirl around the bud that makes me seize on the granite. I lie flat, skin already sprinkled with sweat as he keeps my knees wide to fuck me with his tongue and, oh my God, why did I wait so long to do this?

You waited for Lucas.

Then his lips lock around me. He sucks me into his mouth, tongue flicking over my clit. I scream into the ceiling, the ache in my pussy demanding to be filled with more. He kisses me, stars exploding in my eyes as he blows my fucking mind. I want to sit upright and drag his cock into me, but his tongue is insistent. He doesn't slow down when he feels me clench. If anything, he works at me harder, swirling and licking and sucking. Pleasure coils like a tightly wound spring, but the ache that's buried inside me demands to be set free. I bite my lip, willing to hold the tide back.

Then his rough finger grabs my clit, pinching it as his tongue drives deep.

I come harder than I've ever felt my whole life. All those nights twisted in the sheets. Even the fucking rabbit dildo with all its settings and features doesn't compare to this. Lucas holds me as I ride the crest of the wave, kissing as I clench over and over. Then he pulls away and my legs close against the damp coolness. He lifts me into his arms and carries me.

A creaking sound and the softness pressing against my back tell me we're in his bedroom. I'm still naked. He's still hard. We're going to fuck. This is it.

Just like that, I want him again.

I grab his collar and kiss him, tasting myself but not giving a shit. He kisses me back, his lips softer than I expected. God, I want more of him. I reach for his belt, but he takes my hand and moves it away.

I search his desperate eyes. "What's wrong?"

"You're perfect."

"Then what's the problem?"

His voice softens. "You're going to think I'm nuts." He takes a deep breath. "I don't want you just for the weekend, Alexa. I want you forever."

I sit upright, heart pounding with excitement. "Lucas—"

"I made myself swear I wouldn't touch a woman again until I was sure she wanted to be mine. For good. I'm not in it for a quick fuck, a one-night stand, or even a weekend binge of eating your amazing pussy. I want a wife and kids. I want forever."

His words stir something deep inside me, because I want those things, too. "How do you know I don't want that, too?"

A smile flickers. "You're a virgin."

"Exactly. I've been waiting my whole life to find the right man to give my body to. You're him, I know it."

He touches my cheek. "Maybe you mean it."

"I do."

"And maybe you just me to fuck you."

I do.

A rough timbre enters his voice. "Do you know how hard it is to look at you right now and not touch you? More than anything, I want to be your first. But I need to be your last."

"But I—"

He lays a finger across my lips, silencing me. "Don't make a decision now."

Fire runs through my blood as I watch him sit up, the bed creaking again.

"I'm not going to take your virginity until I know for sure you're mine forever."

CHAPTER EIGHT

Lucas

My entire body aches. It's a good ache, one I haven't felt in a long, long time. Every time I think about Alexa squirming on my bed, my entire body pulses and a dull throb tightens between my legs, desperate for release. I glance over my shoulder and catch her looking at me. She's rolled onto her side, her head propped on my pillow, her body casually thrown across my bed as she recovers. Her sinuous curves silently beg me to come back and finish what I started.

I shouldn't watch her get up, but I do. She rises, arching her back. Her perfect breasts thrust out as she shudders. Barefoot and bare-assed, she walks past me into the living room to find her clothes.

As she passes, she tries desperately not to look, to be a smoldering femme fatale, but she can't keep it up and gives me a nervous glance as though to check if I'm watching. She's on the edge of mastering her sexuality, but there's an urgency to her that betrays the whole thing, and makes her seem young and silly.

It makes me want her even more. Callow, self-interested boys like that Bryan just want to use her until that sweet innocence is tarnished and will never come back.

She puts on a show as she bends to gather her clothes, thrusting herself at me, watching me as she slips her panties back into place.

"Help me, would you?" she asks, her innocent voice betrayed by a quavering anticipation.

I clasp her bra for her, my fingers grazing her warm skin. She takes a step back, rubbing against me as she pulls up her shorts. I slip her shirt over her arms and wrap mine around her to do up the buttons, lingering as I close them over her breasts, feeling the warmth of her against my palms. I button her shirt all the way up to her chin.

Alexa starts undoing them but I trap her hands in mine. "Stop."

"Why?"

I nuzzle her cheek with my lips and savor her gasp as my teeth brush her ear.

"Sometimes it's about what you don't show."

I draw back from her, ignoring the rapid hammering in my chest. The feel of her warmth in my arms and the softness of her hair against my skin is too tempting. I could rip her clothes off as easily as I put them on her.

She crosses her arms as I start gathering my things.

"What are you doing?"

"This is the best time of day for the light. I'm looking for inspiration."

Alexa gives me a crooked smirk, sits on the table in front of the sofa, and starts lacing up her boots. "You're not leaving me here by myself."

"I don't remember saying I was. Are you sure you want to go? The hike can be a little difficult."

"Where are we going?" she asks as she strides to the front door.

I could just watch her move for hours. I've never seen anyone so perfect. Standing by the door, she gathers her thick locks into a loose ponytail. For some reason it makes me even harder for her.

Once I have everything, I open the door and lead her out.

"This way," is all I give her.

She eyes me, but she's trusting, and never asks again as we follow the path along the stream. I cut most of this trail myself, spending months hacking the branches and vines back. Now leaves crunch under our feet, and the air is crisp, heavy with earthy scents.

Alexa stops and gasps as we reach the falls. On the other side of my little homestead there is a sheer drop-off, and the stream has cut a channel into it. The water falls sharply to pool at the bottom before running off in another direction.

"Is this always here?"

"It dries up if there isn't enough rain. You're lucky you weren't here last week. It rained steady for four days."

She marvels at it, and while she is distracted, I watch her. She is most beautiful when she doesn't know, or simply doesn't care that I'm looking.

"I've never seen anything like this before."

"There's a first time for everything," I shrug.

Alexa's eyes widen slightly and her cheeks color. I can practically feel her curling her toes in her boots thinking about it. I should stop teasing her; it's cruel.

"What you said before—" she starts.

I hush her with my finger. She shudders, and her lips part just a bit before I pull my hand away. If I feel them wrapped around my finger I'll start imagining them wrapped around my cock, and then I'll give in. This isn't going anywhere. I'm not going to let her waste something she obviously cares about—no matter how dismissive she sounds—on a silly fling to make herself feel more mature. I want her to remember me fondly.

"Sit on that rock," I tell her, pointing.

"Should I take off my clothes?" she asks with a coy smile.

"Not unless you want to freeze."

"I don't feel the cold when you're watching me."

She gives me a look that matches the suggestion in her voice. She starts roughly unbuttoning her top. It falls on the rock, and then she sheds the rest of her clothes. The afternoon light softens her even more, bringing out her eyes. I watch intently, willing myself not to even blink as she drops her clothes and reveals her curves.

She must have been listening to me. She gives me a thoughtful look and then turns on her seat until she's fully exposed, yet displays nothing. Her arms hide her breasts. A twist of her hip and the position of her legs hides everything else, her thick hair draped down her body.

I sit down on my favorite log and sketch.

"If I sit on this rock too long, you'll have to give me a back rub when we get home."

Home. I shudder when the word passes her lips.

"There aren't any bears or anything out here, are there?" she asks, rubbing her arms.

"Yes," I say. "Coyotes, too."

The look on her face is delectable.

"Well. At least I have you to protect me. I'm sure you'll throw me over your shoulder and carry me off if there's any danger. Seeing as how I'm defenseless and naked."

I smirk, and start working.

She's still visibly tense, despite her earlier bravado. Yet she doesn't complain as I work. The lighting is perfect and she is gorgeous. I have to be careful. Stop my work from edging into the pornographic.

Alexa jumps but makes no sound when she hears the crack of a twig and some rustle of leaves below. She cranes around slowly and then slips off the rock, staring.

The doe gracefully steps to the swirling water at the base of the falls and leans to drink. There's a yearling buck with her, still carrying spots from this spring. Facing away from me, Alexa stares down at them in awe, hands pressed to her chest, her breathing shallow as she forces herself to be still and quiet.

I work as fast as I can, desperate to capture the moment, wincing when my pencils scrape across the paper. This is what I came out here to catch, even if I didn't know it. Alexa makes a little sound and the spell is broken. The doe looks up at her and their eyes meet.

Not in any hurry, but with graceful speed, the deer retreat back into the brush, and Alexa lets out a slow breath, turning to me with wonder in her eyes. For the first time it's like she's truly unaware that she's naked. She's just there, totally confident and innocent at the same time.

God, I have to have her.

The moment lasts a delicious eternity, and then she

flinches as she tries to cover herself and tries not to.

I don't answer her. I just smirk and stand up, helping her dress again. It becomes an embrace as I rub the warmth of my body into her back. She shivers even when her clothes are back on and presses against me while we walk. I end up taking her hand without thinking.

The shadows are long when we reach the cabin again. The bare branches throw sharp, skeletal shadows across the world, reaching for the door.

She rushes inside, and I close it behind her.

"You all right?"

"Yeah, I've just seen too many horror movies about cabins in the woods." She rubs her hands together. "Can you make a fire?"

"Sure."

I cover her shoulders with a blanket. She curls up in it on the couch while I build up a good woodpile and light the kindling.

"Don't you have a heater or something?" she asks.

I shake my head. "I like the cold. I've got a little propane heater so my pipes don't freeze but it's not cold enough for that. Won't be for a week or two more."

"There are other ways to stay warm."

Damn this girl. I'm guessing those other ways involve her naked in my bed, me thrusting into her. Tempting as hell. I pretend that I can't hear the lewd suggestion, even though my brain is seized by an image of me tearing that blanket off her. "Want some hot cocoa?"

She smiles knowingly. "Sure."

I heat the water for the mix on the stove. Alexa watches the blue flames, and the azure light dances in her eyes. It comes to a boil fast enough, and I pour a cup for each of us.

"Marshmallows?" she says, hesitant.

I smirk, and fish the bag out from the drawer. I watch her as I drop them into her cup. She likes it sweet. That doesn't surprise me at all. I keep going until she nods. Her cup is half marshmallow.

She takes it greedily and sips until she burns her tongue. "This is kind of romantic," she says, leaning her head on the back of the sofa.

Alexa kicks out of her boots and stretches her legs onto my lap. I run my hands down her calves. She winces when my fingers dig into the soles of her feet. My hands are cold. She quickly relaxes, though, as I begin kneading them in my hands.

"You will make an amazing husband," she tells me.

I smirk. "We're not getting married. You're staying with me for a few days and modeling for me—"

"When you're not eating my pussy," she interrupts,

smirking. She takes a sip of her cocoa.

"The filthy talk doesn't suit you." Or maybe I can't handle it.

She lets out a fake moan. "Oh, Lucas. Make me come, claim me—"

I'd love to. "Stop it."

She jerks her feet free of my hands and rubs her calves on my lap. Her eyes round. "You're so big. I wonder if you'd fit in my mouth."

You and me both, babe. It takes everything inside me not to give in. "Alexa, if you don't stop, you might get what you wish for."

"Good." She takes a sip of cocoa and pulls her legs from my lap, curling up under the blanket. "I'm right here. I want you."

She sets her cup and saucer aside on the table and crawls to me. I could get up, walk away, make an excuse, but I let her crawl on my lap and straddle me. I do more than let her. My hands slip under her shirt. I savor the shudder when my cool skin presses against her sides, just below her ribs.

Alexa shifts closer, pushed tight so that when my cock hardens from her warmth she can feel it pressing into her. Her kiss is light, a silent invitation delivered with soft lips. I answer it hungrily, diving into her the way I want to dive into her body with my throbbing cock.

"So this is the game. If I get you inside me, I win."

I laugh. "Win what?"

She gives me a shy smile. "You."

Alexa doesn't realize she's already won me over.

She wraps her arms around me, squeezes her breasts to my chest. I forgot how good this feels. There's nothing on Earth quite like holding a lover tight and feeling her breath slow until it matches your own, until we breathe together. My cock is trapped against her. It almost feels like I am inside her already.

Almost. Not quite. The thought of it makes me shudder, makes me kiss her harder.

"I don't want a fling," I tell her, breaking the kiss to taste her throat. "I don't want you to regret this."

"Why would I?"

"Your first time should be meaningful."

She rocks her hips, much as I would want her to if there was nothing between us and I was inside her right now.

"This *is* special. At least one of us knows what he's doing." Her delicate hands curl around the collar of my shirt, tugging lightly. "I want you to teach me. You made me feel so good when you…ate my pussy," she hesitates for just a moment, summoning some deep reserve of

87

bravery.

The innocence she hides behind her fumbling seductions makes me crave her more. I can mold her until I can make her come anytime I please, wring every ounce of pleasure out of her body that she can produce until she passes out. I want her to adore me. I want her to sit in my lap with a big belly. I want to hold her while we watch our children play.

"You're too young for what I want."

She kisses my neck and slips her arms under my shirt. "You don't know that."

"Yes I do, sweetheart. Once upon a time, I was twenty-three and all I could think about was fucking."

"Lucas, I'm not arguing about this with you right now."

"Then—"

"Hold me," she says, nuzzling my neck. "It's cold in here and you're warm."

I hold her. Her hands are freezing against my skin, but I don't mind. "I can't sleep with you."

"Why not?"

"Because if I do, then you'll be mine and I can never let you go." I trace my finger along her chin and cup her face, tilting her head back to kiss her again. "You're too young to be stuck out in the woods being a housewife. It's not what you're for."

I can't stand it anymore. I have to get her off me, but when I start to pull her off my lap she squirms and clamps down with her legs, wriggling loose from my grip as she takes me in hers.

"I'm not letting go," she protests.

"It's been a long day and I need my bed."

"Then you're taking me with you," she purrs. "Even if I have to hang around your neck."

The look in her eyes when I stand up, and make her do just that, is priceless. She locks her legs around my waist and her arms around my neck and clings to me while I walk into the bedroom.

Instead of pushing her off, I hold her tighter. I don't want her to fall.

CHAPTER NINE

Alexa

He's taking me to bed with him.

Giddiness rises in my chest. I feel like a girl again. It's as though it's Christmas morning, and instead of stumbling upon a pile of brightly colored gifts, I'll get to unwrap his package. The one between his legs.

He lets out a grunt as he lets me slide down his arms in the darkness of his bedroom. When my feet hit the floor, I don't move away from him.

In the dark, I can't really see him. I don't know what he's thinking, but I sure as hell know what he's *feeling*.

There's an intake of breath as I let my fingers brush the rigid bump between his legs. "Sorry," I whisper, not sorry at all.

He's silhouetted against the hallway light. "I need to get some shut-eye. If I let you stay in my bed, will you behave?"

No. "Yes. Of course."

He makes a suspicious sound in the back of his throat, and then the floorboards creak. The lamp sitting on his nightstand flares on, illuminating the bedroom in soft, yellow light. It's pretty Spartan as bedrooms go. There's nothing but a bed, two nightstands, and a huge dresser.

Lucas strips the button-up shirt from his back, the sparse light flattering his body. The shadows enhance every dip and crevasse, making his abs look like a maze I'd like to lick my way through. I'm fascinated by his every movement, even the way his muscles roll when he flicks his hand. The shirt flies across the room into a wicker hamper. He opens the sliding doors to his closet where everything is neatly arranged, and then he pulls his jeans down his thick legs. I watch the taut bubble of his ass tighten when he straightens to hang his pants.

In a strange way, the tidiness of the cabin makes me feel insecure. He's not like the hopeless boys at school. Lucas keeps his room neat, launders and irons his own clothes, and cooks. Unlike them, he's capable. He doesn't want to use me like a mom he's allowed to fuck.

I glance at the empty nightstand on the right. Once it was filled with her personal things. Whoever she is. He could've easily thrown it out, turned it into splinters with that axe of his, but he kept it empty. As if he were waiting for the right person to come along so he could fill it again.

He wants a wife. A partner. I understand now.

Feeling returns to my limbs when he moves to his side of the bed and slides beneath the covers. He makes a line in the middle of the bed with his arm, casually lying on the comforter.

I approach the bed, pulling the shirt from my body. Lucas' eyes devour me as I unclasp my bra and let myself loose. I bend over, my breasts a teardrop shape as I stick my fingers behind the waistband of my jeans and pull down. There's nothing but a thin piece of cotton guarding the heat between my legs.

"What the hell do you think you're doing?"

I look up. "Getting ready for bed."

"You need to do that with your tits all out?"

I smile to myself. "It's uncomfortable to wear a bra."

He balls the sheets in his fists. "Alexa, don't make me regret letting you sleep here."

"Oh, you won't."

Lucas doesn't miss the coyness in my voice. He gives me a sharp look. "I have plans for you, babe. If you curl up next to me with your tits pressed against my arm, all those plans will go out the window, and I don't want that."

"You don't?"

"No," he says, a trace of annoyance creeping into his voice. "Come here."

A thrill runs down my spine as his command cracks through the room. I walk to the bed, peeling back the covers. My knees sink into the mattress as I crawl into bed, and all the while Lucas' eyes are trained on to mine, filling me with heat.

His fingers curl around my jaw, and I expect him to manhandle me. Throw me down on the bed. Crush his lips against mine. But that's not Lucas. The only sign of his waning restraint is in the way his eyes shift like burning coals.

"Alexa," he says, breathing my name over my lips. "I'm not going to pop your cherry until I'm sure you know what you're signing up for."

Is he insane? "I *do* know."

"No, you don't, because I'm not interested in meaningless sex. If that was all I was after, I would've tied you to my bed the moment you trespassed on my property and had my way with you."

My heart beats faster as I open my mouth to tell him that sounds fantastic, but he's still talking.

"I don't want to fuck you and send you on your way."

Then I force myself to speak, voice cracking. "I don't want that either."

"Hold on, I'm not finished. There's something else I need." Then warmth brushes my stomach as he moves his hand lower to cup me. "A family."

My heart thumps again, harder this time. A rush of blood floods my brain as Lucas' intoxicating scent swirls around me.

He stares at me, his eyes hard now. "Do you honestly think you can handle that?"

Can I handle letting him fill me with his seed, my belly growing huge with his child—*our* child? Can I handle a life with him forever, in this cabin? My heart says yes. Undoubtedly, yes.

"Of course I could. Lucas, you realize those are all things I want, too, right? I'm twenty-three years old. I want a husband and kids just like everyone else."

"But you've never had a man. You're going to need to do a lot more to convince me you know what you're getting into."

His hand drops from my face, and he turns away to reach the lamp.

What does he mean by that? How am I supposed to convince him that I'm serious about wanting him to be my first and last lover?

I know it sounds crazy. Lucas and I met only a couple days ago. To the casual observer, I am off my fucking rocker for taking a leap of faith like this. Trusting a man I barely know to be my husband and father my children. Hell, even wanting a man you hardly know to do all those things is bizarre. There's no question that if one of my friends told me she was considering eloping with a man she just met, I would've told her: No. Wait a few years. Why rush?

But it's different when you meet someone and everything feels right, way more than it should for the first date. And you know deep in your bones that this is the man you're supposed to end up with. You'll go anywhere, so long as it's with him. That's how I feel about Lucas, and I can't explain it.

I just know.

So I slide my hand around his waist and cuddle up behind him, folding my body into his, and then I wrap my fingers around the thickness jutting against his black boxers.

Lucas turns around lazily with a small smile, as though he expected this. "You are so begging for it."

I look straight at him. "I'm trying to convince you that I'm serious about you."

And how does a girl do that? By giving him a fantastic blowjob.

He watches as I swing my leg over his waist, shimmying down until I'm face-to-face with his groin. I lean down, kissing a patch of skin right above his boxers. Instead of pulling away, my lips move down. Then I press them against his growing hardness. His fingers dig into my hair.

"Wrapping your lips around my cock is not what I meant about convincing me, sweetheart."

I freeze, mouth hovering over him. It wasn't what he meant, but that doesn't mean he'd say no to a blowjob. "You tasted me," I say, slowly tugging his boxers. "Now I want to taste you."

He heaves a great sigh. "You fucking temptress. We're still doing things my way, honey. No sex. Not until you're mine."

"I'm in your bed, Lucas."

He lifts his hips as he glares at me for daring to tempt him. I pull his boxers off, gazing at his cock for the first time. It's warm in my hand. I grab the root of him. He's so thick with blood I can feel his heartbeat pounding. Amazed by the smoothness of his skin, I glide up his length and swirl my thumb over his bulbous head. Lucas sucks in a breath.

I smile at him. "A good wife should know how to give head, shouldn't she?"

He says nothing, looking at me with a mixture of lust and fury. I bend down, intoxicated with the power I have over him. Then I breathe him in. Nothing. My tongue darts out for a taste. A pleasant, slightly salty taste. I allow my tongue to flatten against him, swirling on his underside. I'm no stranger to blowjobs. Giving my mouth to men never mattered to me. The rest of me? That was for the man I'd meet one day, not the boys I tolerated to get experience.

I wrap my lips around him and feel him bulging in my throat as I take him deep. Lucas' firm hold has become a caress, his nails gentle against my skin. I feel him buck his hips as I glide up and down his length. He moans when he buries himself deep enough to hit my throat. Damn, that's hot. I twist my head, swirling my tongue around the tip and hard against his underside, flicking against that sensitive spot. His grip becomes hard, punishing. He fucks my mouth. I love it.

And when I look up into Lucas' feverish gaze, I know that he's going to come in my mouth. When it happened with anyone else, I excused myself to the bathroom and spat it out, always feeling like a dirty little whore when I looked at myself in the mirror. This is different. He told me he wanted more than just a quick fuck, and by taking him between my lips I accepted that.

His fingers tighten as he grinds his hips against my lips. The room echoes with his guttural moan as he finishes inside me. I feel him tense, and then a fantastic warmth fills my mouth. I swallow him as he pumps a few more times, more jets hitting the back of my throat. Shaking, he parts the hair from my face and I make sure to suck every drop from his cock. He pops from my lips, still hard as nails.

He kisses me. Long and hard, as though we're lovers who were separated for years. He sucks in my bottom lip and bites down, hard enough to make me yelp. When he pulls back, he massages my lip as though in apology. I want him so badly I can taste my arousal, thick in the air.

I don't know what he's thinking. "Did you like it?"

He lets out a sigh. "I don't think I'll ever forget the image of your perfect lips wrapped around me. You're incredible. So innocent."

The last word breathes against my mouth before it's cut off by my kiss. I want him so bad I could shift my panties and sit on his erect cock. He ends the kiss before I can try.

"Get some sleep, Alexa. We've got a lot to do tomorrow."

"Okay." Then I feel like a foolish girl for thinking I could convince him with a blowjob. Who do I think he is? He's not some jerk who'll be swayed by the first girl who gets on her knees for him.

I burrow deep into the bed when Lucas flips the light off. I think he's going to ignore me the whole night, but then I hear the bed groan, and his body presses against my back. A leaping feeling spreads through my stomach when his arm snakes around my waist and holds me to his chest.

His head buries in my neck, another leap of excitement, and then he whispers, "Two days, Alexa. Sleep well."

* * *

Two days until I leave? Two days until he decides whether I want to be his wife or not? Until he fucks me? What in the hell did he mean? I obsess over it all night when I'm supposed to be sleeping. How can I when my skin burns at his closeness?

When dawn filters through the cracks in the trees, I slide Lucas' arm off my body and gently ease out of bed. He's still lost in sleep, gorgeous even when he's knocked out. I open the drawers in the dresser by the bed, finding half of them empty, until I see a pile of T-shirts. I grab a white one and pull it over my head. It's so long that it covers me to mid-thigh.

My toes curl against the cold floor, but I find I'm getting used to it. I walk into the living room and smile at the unwashed mug of cocoa sitting near the sink. I think about us curled up on the couch, his hand stroking my growing belly. It's a nice image.

A soft knock at the door pops the glow of my vision. I hesitate, not wanting to wake Lucas up. Should I answer it? My hand hovers at the doorknob. Finally I grab it.

I open it a crack and, recognizing Jess' wild, black curls,

I open it farther. "What are you doing here?"

She looks at my bare legs and the shirt, which I realize is probably translucent. Her mouth opens in shock. "Holy shit, you fucked this guy?"

"Would you keep your voice down?"

She does, a smirk widening her face. "Alexa Monroe, I'm impressed. You had rando sex. Good for you!"

"No, I didn't."

"Like hell!"

"Not that it's any of your business, but I didn't sleep with him. Well, we did sleep in the same—"

"Oh please, would you stop trying to justify it? I don't give a damn who you give your v-card to. I'm just here to tell you we're leaving early." She rolls her eyes. "Turns out the boys can't handle the cold, and Bryan's been bitching at me ever since you gave him the cold shoulder—oh my God, does your mountain man have art on his walls?"

I look over my shoulder. "Yeah, he's a bit of an artist."

"A bit?" She grabs the edge of the door, opening it wider. "Wow. He's a collector?"

"No, it's all his work," I say, seizing the moment to gush about Lucas. "He's brilliant."

"Oh my God, I have to see this."

"No, wait—"

She pushes her way through before I can stop her.

Sighing, I keep the door open even though the frigid cold keeps rolling in. Headstrong is Jess' middle name. So is Pain in the Ass.

"Wow!" She takes off her hat as though she's walking through the Sistine Chapel. She gazes around at all the still lifes, portraits, and watercolor paintings. "This is amazing, Alexa. You hit the jackpot."

"I think he's too good for me, honestly."

"Hell no, Alexa. You find a man like this and you take him and *run*. I'd ditch Greg in a second for a man with talent like this."

This is making me nervous. She really shouldn't be in here, and I doubt Lucas would appreciate a stranger poking through his things. "Look, I really think you should leave."

"Holy crap, this is beautiful. Wait, is this you?" Jess peels back the piece of paper hiding the canvas sketch of me on the easel, her mouth wide with shock. "Lucas Wood—am I reading this signature right?"

"Yeah, that's his name. What? You don't approve now?"

I'm bewildered by the hostile look she throws my way. "Fuck you."

"What's your problem?'

"You spread your legs for Lucas Wood! He told you

he'd help you get an art gallery, didn't he?"

Fury balls in my chest. "I don't know what the hell you're getting at, but you are way out of line."

"I'm out of line. Right." She steps back, laughing. "You're fucking *Lucas Wood*. One of the greatest artists of our generation. They featured him in our contemporary art class. You seriously expect me to believe you didn't recognize him?"

A flicker of a memory dances in my mind, slightly out of reach. It feels like a million years ago when I was worried about a photograph. Goddamn it. "It's not like that," I say too quickly. "We're not having sex. I haven't asked him for any favors."

"That's why you wanted to come here, wasn't it?" she shouts, not bothering to keep quiet now. "You wanted to find Lucas-Fucking-Wood. You fuck him, and he hands you a spot in a gallery."

"No, that's not true!"

"I can't believe you!" she roars. "All that shit about how you're a virgin, and you give it to the first man who's willing to trade you something for it. Guess what, that doesn't make you smart. It makes you a fucking whore."

A deeper voice cracks through the room like thunder. "You need to get the hell out."

I look behind me, eyes stung with tears, and Lucas is

standing in the living room, arms crossed. His face is white with fury for Jess, but he looks at me and his eyes soften.

CHAPTER TEN

Lucas

There is an intruder in my home. The door stands open, letting the early morning chill flood inside. It raises gooseflesh on Alexa's legs, making her shiver. Her back is straight and she's furious, staring down her friend, who has tracked mud into my house with her ridiculous leather boots.

"Get the hell out," I bark again.

Alexa flinches and takes a halting half step until she bumps into me while her friend glowers. Beyond the door, Bryan lurks. The way he takes advantage of Alexa's state of undress to get an eyeful is starting to piss me off. She folds her arms over her chest and her toes curl like she's trying to suck her bare legs up into her shirt.

"Hey," I snap at the boy. "Keep your eyes to yourself."

Bryan shoves his fists in his pockets and turns away, defeated.

Alexa's friend, or ex-friend, smirks at me. "It doesn't hurt that he's hot. Hope you enjoy fucking your way into fame, Alexa."

Alexa glares back, silent. The girl struts out of my

house and pulls the door shut behind her with a slam.

I turn the dead bolt so hard it feels like the knob will shear off in my hand, and turn around. Alexa takes another step back, this time away from me. Her eyes are wet with the threat of tears. She shakes her head.

"Monday?" I ask.

Alexa sighs. "Yeah. They came to tell me they're going back early. We were supposed to stay through the weekend but I guess they got tired of country living."

Turning, she looks up at me, apprehension in her eyes. "Listen," she says.

I put my arms on her shoulders and pull her in, drawing her into a gentle embrace.

Her whole body shakes. "I'm not trying to get anything out of you. I promise."

"Be quiet."

She tenses, sucking in a breath to plug up any more explanations. I stroke the back of her head and caress her back.

"It's cold. Let's get you warmed up."

I guide her back into the bedroom and swaddle her in my robe. It's about four sizes too big for her and more like a blanket. She wraps it around and around herself until she's a formless roll of flannel with a pretty, smiling face sticking out.

"What she said is not true," Alexa says, an edge still in her voice.

"I know," I assure her, holding her.

"I don't want anything from you but you."

I press my lips to her forehead. "When a girl looks at you with your cock in her mouth the way you did last night, you know she's a keeper."

She laughs and playfully smacks my chest. "Don't be nasty."

I laugh at her, loudly. "You're telling me not to be dirty? Miss Oh, fuck me, Lucas."

Suddenly we're on the bed and I'm on top of her, kissing her. She shakes her legs loose of my robe and wraps them around my waist, pulling me in. It would be so easy to shuffle my shorts down and thrust inside her, but I stop myself with aching restraint.

I roll off her, leaving her lying there in my splayed-out robe, my borrowed shirt hiked up to her waist to bare her long legs. She shamelessly displays the soft petals of her pussy. Her stomach tenses a little to lift her hips and invite me to a different sort of breakfast.

I touch her mound just above her clit and run my finger up to her belly button before walking out of the bedroom.

A drawer thumps and she emerges wearing a pair of my

boxers, knotted at the small of her back to keep them up. She brushes past me into the kitchen, where she grabs a pan, lightly humming to herself.

"What are you doing?"

"Making breakfast," she announces.

I fold my arms. She gives me a smirk.

"When I said I wanted a partner I didn't mean a maidservant."

"That's too bad. I bet you'd love it if I wore one of those little outfits with the black dress and white lace. Ooh la la."

Her smirk turns into a grin and she begins cracking eggs into a mixing bowl. "I cook for myself."

"Can't you just let me be nice to you?"

I swallow. "Nobody has cooked for me in a long time. I'm not really used to it."

She bites her lips and her pretty face is briefly clouded with worry. "What else do you want?"

I lay my hand on her lovely thick ass and squeeze.

She snickers. "That's not on the menu right now."

"Make up your mind."

She smirks.

"I'll help," I insist. "You make the eggs, I'll make the toast and the bacon."

It takes some getting used to, the presence of another

person in my little domain. I keep turning around expecting to flip the eggs myself, but she's there, humming as she whisks them in the pan with the spatula. I don't know the tune, but it sounds oddly familiar.

When the plates are on the counter, she picks up her stool and moves it next to mine so we're almost touching as we eat. She snatches a piece of bacon off my plate and I glare at her.

"Are you trying to provoke me?"

"Maybe," she says. "What are we going to do today? Another nature walk? More nude modeling?"

The promise in her eyes almost makes me say yes.

I roll my shoulders. "We'll see. Have to clean up after ourselves first."

Alexa fills my home. I find myself stopping to stare at her as she does the most mundane things, like scrubbing her dish in the sink. The way the light from the window fills her hair, the way she leans forward just so, presenting the inviting curves of her back and her luscious ass in an unconscious, innocent way.

I step behind and press into her, reaching into the sink to help her clean. She rubs her ass against me, and I press my chest into her back. Doing the dishes turns into an erotic dance that makes me harder with every second that passes.

I can't stand it anymore. As she dries her hands I wrap my arms around her, trap her in my embrace, and dip her backward to lock my lips on hers. She squirms and relaxes in my arms until I stand her back up.

"What was that for?"

I stroke my fingers down her chin. "Get dressed."

She heads for the bedroom and grabs my hand to pull me along. This time she is demure. She hides herself as she disrobes, showing me only glimpses of the outer curves of her breasts, turning so I only see her legs and hips as she steps into her panties and pulls them up. A half-turn, and she looks over her shoulder, her eyes meeting mine.

"Are you going to get dressed, or stare at me?" she says. "Maybe I should take these clothes back off?"

"I'm starting to wonder if I should bother letting you dress at all."

That got her. She shivers just slightly, and I can tell from her eyes that if I told her to strip right now she'd do it.

I smirk and change my clothes. She watches. I like it. Feeling her gaze on my skin, I think about the feeling of her sucking my cock last night. The shocking heat of her mouth, the softness of her lips, the look in her eyes. That most of all.

Alexa strides out of the bedroom and into the living

room. I watch, savoring her every movement. She sinks into the couch and crosses her legs, fidgeting nervously. I don't know why she's gone from seductive to tense so fast.

I take a seat beside her. The couch is old and I bought it secondhand, so my weight on the creaky springs all but dumps her in my lap. She lifts her legs over my lap and wraps around my body, her head on my shoulder.

"Can we talk?" she says.

I wait. There is a terrible, sharp twist in my stomach— this is where she tells me it's great but she has to go back to her life.

"I'm supposed to leave soon, but I don't want to. I want to stay."

My fingers wander to her neck and I toy with her hair, lightly twisting her locks around my fingers.

Savor this. Let her stay as long as she wants. I did it. I've won.

"What if I don't go back? What if I just stay here with you?"

"Think about what you'd be giving up if you do that."

"Giving up?" she says, then snorts. "What would that be? My crappy cliquey friends and their bullshit? Cooking for my bitchy roommate who doesn't even thank me?"

She glides across my lap and straddles me. "I've finally found someone who appreciates me. I want to be yours forever. In every way."

It's hard to think with all the blood rushing from my head. My hands want to do the talking. I start to wonder how I'll get anything done if she stays. I can't stop touching her. I lose myself in the softness of her hair, the heat of her body, the weight of her in my lap.

Pulling her close, I bring my mouth to her ear.

"I want more than a wife and children. I want you to be my wife, and have my children. I want this life, and you to be part of it. Think long and hard, Alexa. I'm not going to decide to move to a city loft or whatever else. I'm not going back to surrounding myself with frauds and con artists."

She starts to speak. I silence her with a kiss.

"Come with me."

She smirks at the double entendre as I take her by the waist and lift her off my lap. She presses close as I stand, my body gliding against hers as I rise to my feet. I don't know how much longer I can stand it. She puts her hands on my belt. I pull her wrists away and caress her palms with my thumbs.

I need her now.

Taking her hand, I lead her outside. She gathers her hair behind her neck as she walks, tying a loose ponytail.

Leading her behind the cabin, I take her to the storage

shed I built but never used. The padlock is rusted shut, and it takes me some grunting effort to get it loose. Alexa watches, her eyes guarded. I motion her inside.

I flick the switch and the bare lightbulb overhead shivers to life. The light is pale and harsh but Alexa is beautiful anyway. It makes her ghostly and ethereal. The image is haunting, another to inspire me again.

The work shed was built with a bench fixed to the wall, and there's enough room for her to set up everything she'd need.

She looks around the room for a moment, then her eyes light up. She looks at me and claps. "Is this for me?"

I step forward. "It is now. You need a darkroom, don't you?"

She nods, grinning. "It's perfect. It needs some cleaning up."

I eye her. "How about some gratitude?"

Alexa throws herself in my arms and twists, turning her back against my body. I lean on her a little.

"We can make this your place," I tell her. "It'll take a little work to get it in shape. Oh, and a red bulb."

She wriggles against me. "Oh, we can work on it. I'm already picturing you all sweaty with tools in your hands."

I take her hand, lightly rubbing her ring finger with my thumb.

"Stay with me. Marry me. Have my children."

She takes a deep breath.

"I didn't know how much I wanted someone to say that to me until I met you. Yes. Yes, Lucas. I'll marry you, whatever you want."

"I hoped you'd say that."

She spins and grabs my belt.

"If we're going to make a baby, we should get started," she says, an eager grin on her face.

I cup her cheeks in my hands. "You should know by now, I like taking my time."

She quivers, a small pulse of excitement against my palms. My hands fall down her arms, move to her sides. Alexa lets out a little yelp when I lift her bodily from the floor and set her on the workbench. Her legs reach out and wrap around me, drawing me in.

My hand slips inside her jeans, skimming along the inward curve of her firm stomach and between her legs to the stunning softness of her. She makes a small noise and hugs closer to me while my finger sinks inside her.

Fuck. She grips me as I slip deeper, slick and warm. The feeling of her body wrapped around me drives me insane, my heart pounding like a timpani.

Alexa grips my collar in her hands until her knuckles turn white, her eyes pleading with me as I pump my finger inside her, stroking her from within. She squirms and bucks in my embrace, her thighs squeezing my hand, trapping it.

"Just like that," she breathes, her voice choked with pleasure.

Her fists shake against my skin. Her delectable wetness slicks my hand, her thighs. We find a rhythm, my hand and her hips, and she curls up against me and bucks, crying out so loud it shakes little streamers of dust from the roof over our heads. I swear she could break my fingers, she's gripping me so tight, quivering pulses running down her body as she slumps in my arms.

"Lucas," she says, my name a prayer on her lips.

"I'm taking you inside."

I'm going to tear off her clothes. I'm going to make art, and I'm going to make love. When I'm done with her, Alexa will never want to leave my side.

She gazes at me with longing and I imagine holding her with a swollen belly, my seed taken root inside her. A life, a family, a future.

I can't hold back anymore. I have to have her.

"I'm going to make you remember your first time forever."

CHAPTER ELEVEN

Alexa

My skin tingles with a thousand needlelike sensations as Lucas holds me against his chest, lifting me in the air like I weigh nothing. My jeans are still undone, the fly unzipped when he shoved his hand down my pants and thrust his fingers inside me. It didn't take long for me to come all over his hands. Part of me is embarrassed, but Lucas' heated smile isn't mocking.

"W-where are we going?"

He carries me out of the photography studio, which looks like an ordinary shed from the outside. He could've used it for a million different things, but he's giving it to me. My own darkroom.

I bury my face into his neck against the sting of the cold.

"We're going to make art, Alexa," he whispers into the shell of my ear.

"Together?" I ask, heart beating fast. "Like, we're going to draw?"

He chuckles a bit as he heaves the door to the cabin open. "Something like that."

The grittiness in this voice leaves a lot to the imagination. I'm pretty sure he's not talking about us

115

taking turns sketching on a piece of canvas.

I curl my toes when we enter the warmth of his house. He carries me down the hall. I suck in my breath when we pass his bedroom, but Lucas keeps walking to a room I've never been to before.

Old bedsheets cover the floor of the small room, which is surrounded by four blank walls. There's a white palette sitting on the floor next to a giant piece of canvas lying flat on the ground. Tubs of nontoxic paint are arranged in a neat row beside the palette.

"What is this?"

He sets me down gently but doesn't remove his hands from my waist. "I set it up for you, Alexa."

I gaze at the tubs of paint and the canvas. *We're going to make art, Alexa.* His voice booms in my head, tinged with a sultry, deep growl. The breath catches in my throat when he steps back, a grin hitched on his rugged face when he pulls his T-shirt from his back.

Oh my God. He's going to take my virginity.

Heat rushes to my face when I'm finally confronted with his plans. Excitement sparks up and down my spine as a half-naked Lucas approaches me, his bulge already thick against his jeans.

He slides his hands up my arms. "Ever since you told me you were a virgin, I've been thinking about how I'd make your first time special." His touch becomes protective. "I wanted you naked on that canvas, covered in paint while I fucked you."

Arousal rolls in the air, thick and heady between my legs. My lips part as Lucas lowers his face to mine. His mouth grazes my jaw. "How does that sound?"

"Amazing," I manage to whisper. "I can't think of anything more perfect."

"I can," he says, eyes blazing. "Say you'll be with me forever. Tell me you want to build a life with me. Promise me, and I'm yours."

I think of waking up every morning, enclosed in these cozy walls, married to *him*. Lucas Wood. The man who inspires awe inside me every day. Who dotes on me. Supports my creativity. Loves me.

We'll make art together.

Yes, we will.

I can't get the words out fast enough. "Of course I'll be your wife. It's all I ever wanted."

A real smile staggers across his face. "Then take off your clothes."

I want him so badly my fingers are shaking as I take off the white T-shirt drowning my naked body. He looks at me with a man's hunger, and a thrill hits my chest when he removes the last barrier between us.

His black briefs drop to the floor soundlessly, revealing his thick cock. He takes my hand and lets me wrap my fingers around him. God, it's so rigid. *Huge.* A tiny sliver of panic hits me. How on earth am I going to fit this inside me?

He lets out a small chuckle, wrapping his huge arm around my back. "Don't worry, Alexa. I'll go easy on you."

The air between us feels different—electrified. My skin tingles as his gaze wanders down my body, as if he can't decide which part to claim first. I squeeze him, loving the way his eyelashes flutter against his cheeks. Sucking in a quick breath, he takes my wrists and guides me to the floor.

"Come here, Alexa." I follow him to the stretch of canvas, and he kneels down beside me. I watch him as he selects one of the pots—a blue one. He unscrews the plastic lid, revealing a rich cobalt. "Don't worry, the paint is perfectly safe."

"I trust you."

He smiles. Then he dips two fingers inside. The paint coats them thickly as he removes his hand and slathers one of my boobs with it. I gasp as the cool liquid touches my skin. A thick smear of blue spreads across the underside, and Lucas dips his hand in the tub for more. This time he pools it in his hand and gropes me, his thumb massaging my nipple in slow, sensual circles. He rolls the paint between his thumb and my skin, making sure it's coating me, and doubling as an erotic massage. I lie flat against the canvas, my knees already open for him. He kisses my neck and I hear the sound of more liquid.

Shocking pink slathers my abdomen. His hand moves in broad strokes, soaking my hips with paint, my inner thighs, leaving my pussy untouched. My legs wrap around his waist as he works, nearly bursting with my need for him. "Lucas—"

"Hush, we're almost done." He offers me a tub of red paint. The playful grin dancing on his face couldn't stretch any wider. "Tag me."

I take it and color his biceps with red. Heart pounding, I slather it all over his chest and even run streaks over his muscled thighs. We're both bright with colors by the time I'm done, and then I put it aside. A carnal look descends over his features.

This is it.

His breath comes out ragged as a broad pressure touches between my legs. "Alexa," he breathes into my mouth. "I'm not wearing a condom."

"Oh." My heart pounds against my chest. "I'm not on any birth control."

I expect him to pull away. To stand up. Instead he stays

there, his eyes deepening with lust. "Good," he says, and a thrill runs through me. "I said I wanted forever, Alexa. I meant it, and I want to start by making a baby with you."

The question is there, burning in his gaze. He wants to empty his seed inside me, fill me up with his essence so it can hopefully take root and—make a baby. It sounds crazy, but something primal in my body wants it. Yes, even wants the vision of my belly swelling to come true.

"Let's make a baby," I whisper.

He touches my face, all tender. Then he pushes.

I gasp as the broadness slides an inch inside me, gripped tight by my muscles. He waits, watching my face intently, and buries himself a little deeper. I'm overwhelmed by the feeling. He's warm, so thick that it hurts. Something deep inside me cries out when he pushes all the way in, anchored inside me. Soft lips touch mine, swallowing my gasp. He pulls out—God, I can feel myself gripping him—and then he sinks back inside. Each time he thrusts a little harder. My wetness coats him all the way around, and it starts to feel *amazing*.

This is what it's like.

It's incredible. Even when I listened to Jess go on and on about her boyfriends and rolled my eyes when she bragged about how good it felt, I had no idea. It's better than chocolate. Nothing beats a real man's throbbing cock, the smell of his hair, his sweat clinging to my skin, the way my body flames when he touches me. Nothing.

I cling to his neck, digging in as his hips wetly smack against mine. Then his tongue swirls in my mouth, and I'm jarred back with the intensity of his thrusts. Lucas pulls back, wildness dancing over his face. His cock slides out, and I'm left clenching at the air until he grabs my hips and flips me facedown on the canvas. My hands make red palm prints.

"Spread your knees," he barks.

I obey him, legs trembling when his body seals against the backs of my thighs. He rolls his cock up my slicked pussy and slides right in. Lucas makes a primal sound, a grunt at the back of his throat. Rough hands curve around my hips, holding me against him as he thrusts hard. My knees slide over the canvas, spreading paint everywhere. I'm knocked to my forearms as he fucks me with an intensity that thrills me. He's no longer a man—he's a beast fueled by the need to fuck and impregnate his mate. His arm wraps around me, lifting my ass so he can drive in deep. My boobs make blue orbs on the canvas.

Every thrust satiates that need I've always felt aching inside me. His hand gropes for my pussy and then he pinches my clit, making the space tighter and amping up my pleasure. Oh my God. His cock glides inside me, rubbing against that bed of nerves I always strived to hit with my dildo. As my breathing rises to a hitch, he kisses my back and increases his pace.

"Come for me, Alexa!"

He presses down hard, rubbing my clit in a circle that finally shoves me over the edge. I cry out, my pussy clenching all over him. At the same time his grunts become more feverish and his hands more rough, jerking me back. Then I feel him come. It's the most incredible thing in the world.

His cock stiffens inside me as he anchors in, and then he sighs long and hard. Hot jets fill me with his cum as he pushes it deep. Another thrust. Another release. I'm so wet and full by the time he's done, his legs shaking with exertion.

Lucas wraps his arm around my waist and pulls out of me. Then he gathers me in his embrace, tipping my head toward his. His kiss makes my heart do backflips, and when we separate I see a glow in his eyes.

"You took my innocence," I say with a laugh. "How does it feel?"

He brushes my cheek. "I doubt I could ever do that." His lips touch mine and he squeezes me, making me melt all over again.

"Do you think I'm pregnant?"

I've never seen him look so happy. "No idea. It might take us a few tries to make a family."

A family. The word hits me in the chest. "When can we try again?"

"I should probably leave you alone for a couple days. You'll be sore for a while."

I am, but that doesn't mean I want him to hold off. "There's no way I can stay away from you for days. I don't care how much it hurts."

A pleasant rumble echoes from his chest. "Be patient, Alexa." His hand brushes my stomach. He looks at it in wonder, as though he can already imagine the baby growing inside it.

I can't believe it. A baby. This is really going to happen. "You should probably meet my parents before we get married. They're going to freak."

"We can handle it together."

Then I know that my instinct was right about him. The first moment I saw him, I was caught up in awe. Now I can't imagine a life without him.

And I'll never have to again.

CHAPTER TWELVE

Lucas

I've heard it said plenty of times that pregnant women glow. I have never known it to be true. I've met my share of couples with a baby on the way. In another life. It feels like a distant memory. Bellies would swell and babies would appear and the truth was, there was nothing magical about it.

Until Alexa.

She glows. She fills the room with her presence, makes the air crackle with her spirit and the presence of the child growing inside her. My child. Her hand never leaves her stomach.

Her radiance is undiminished. My desire for her has not faded. I feel a stir every time I look at her, and another every time I look at the canvas.

The creation we produced together that afternoon in the cabin is not the only work I've created since Alexa stumbled into my life. Half a dozen hang suspended from the ceiling. Mingled with them are Alexa's photographs, elegantly composed, some in black and white, some candid, almost blurry, spur of the moment snaps. The gallery has become a tribute to our life together.

I stand beside her and sip champagne. It's a shame she can't have any. We have so much to celebrate. I thought the day she told me she was pregnant would be the happiest day of my life, but every day gets happier still.

That moment is etched in my mind. She looked like an angel, her hand pressed to her still-flat stomach, grinning from ear to ear before she pounced on me. Her lust hadn't diminished at all.

I want her now more than ever. I shouldn't spend our grand opening hovering over my wife, but the temptation is irresistible and I have to rest my hand on hers for a moment and kiss the top of her head.

The painting has a similar effect on her. She keeps looking at it and every time she does, a little more color enters her cheeks. She bites down on a giggle, her jaw quivering like she's shaking the life out of the laughter before it escapes her lips.

A light buzzing fills the air. There are far more people here than I thought. They may have mocked me as a painter of cereal boxes and movie posters behind my back, but the art world has noticed Lucas Wood's triumphant return. They turned out for the unveiling of *Nude by Afternoon Light*. There are a dozen photographers in front of us, crowding around it.

Alexa leans over to me. "This is so hot."

I loop my arm around her waist as a rush of blood fills my cock. "I didn't know you had an exhibitionist streak."

"I didn't have quite a few things in me until I met you."

I smirk and take her hand, fiddling with her ring. Alexa was hesitant to accept an engagement ring at all. What did it matter about some piece of jewelry when we'd already created life together? I insisted, just something modest. I want her marked. I want to declare to the world that she's mine.

"It's magnificent," one of the guests says,

standing next to us. "I never realized you had this level of technique, Wood. I'm simply floored. I feel myself endlessly drawn into it."

Do I know this guy? I think he snuffed at one of my works in another gallery all those years ago. I can't really remember.

"The orbs in the center," he says. "That's a nod to Aphrodite, isn't it?"

It's a nod to my wife's fabulous tits. "Hmm," is all I say.

He raises a glass in his hand and strides off to mingle. Alexa almost has to bite her hand to stop from laughing.

"Orbs," she says.

"Orbs," I repeat. "I like that."

She jabs her elbow into my side. "Tits, boobs, knockers, fun bags, anything but orbs."

I give her ass a discreet squeeze. "If you say so."

Leaving her is like tearing out a clump of hair. I don't let her know how much I fret over her now. She really is drinking white grape juice, and sipping it at that; she has loudly and frequently informed me how much she has to pee now, and how it is absolutely my fault.

It's not her that worries me. Some deep instinctive urge keeps me focused on her, always shifting so Alexa is in the fringes of my vision, like the first light promising a sunrise on a warm day. That's when I'm not outright looking at her, protective anger surging in my chest anytime someone gets too close to Alexa.

I can barely wait. I'm almost afraid my heart will burst when I see my son in her arms. Just the thought of it is so beautiful it swallows everything else and I realize someone was talking to me.

Startled, I make some excuses and work my way back over to her, and take her hand. Alexa smiles warmly and leans in close.

"I need a break."

We built the gallery in the shell of an old repair shop. It gave it plenty of character, as well as a second floor reached by a winding spiral staircase of wrought iron. It's perfectly safe, but I still hold her by the waist as she walks up.

Other women lose some grace in their walk, but Alexa sways. Everything about her is more her. It goes beyond the physical. There's a deeper glow in her skin, her breasts are fuller, her entire form more feminine and seductive, but she's even more than that. Glow is the only word to describe it.

Up here there's nothing but our offices. We still work out in the cabin and are planning to operate the gallery by appointment only. The next exhibition will feature some local artists, and Alexa's photography of their work and their process.

She leans on the cast-iron railing and looks down, letting out a slow breath. I stand behind her and rest my hands on her stomach.

"How do you think it's going?"

"It's going well. They're heaping praise on us. We don't need the money, but we can entertain offers if you like."

She shrugs.

I move my hands up, toward her chest.

Alexa sighs and gently grips my wrists. "We're with people. No boob grabbing."

I push up a little anyway, and she giggles.

"I swear I will make you go on a peanut-butter-cup and pickle-sandwich run again if you don't stop."

I settle for resting my hands on her belly and my chin on her head. She pushes back and molds herself against me, and without really meaning to, the two of us rock from side to side.

"I love you," I murmur.

"I love you, too, Lucas," she says, grinning. "You don't have to tell me every day. I don't doubt you."

"Yes I do."

Something pulses against my hand. I flinch, my eyes widening slightly. Alexa tenses for a moment then laughs, rubbing my hands.

"Your son just kicked me," she says.

"I'll have a talk with him about respecting his mother when he comes out."

I lead her back down, ignoring the way she

rolls her eyes at my caution, and rejoin the party. Her friends showed up, but Alexa hasn't talked to them. I didn't invite any from my old social circle, only the necessary professional contacts.

It doesn't matter. My universe revolves around her. The rest is just buzzing in my ears until it's time to send everyone home. I lock up the gallery and give her a boost up into my truck, and we drive back to the cabin.

Very carefully.

"I could get out and run faster than this," Alexa snorts.

* * *

It's our first day back.

Three weeks before Alexa's due date, we took up residence in an Airbnb in town, to be closer to the hospital when the time came. We spent an extra two weeks after, while we welcomed little Aiden into the world.

I've been working furiously to keep the place warm. My hands are more calloused than ever from hewing the firewood, but Alexa doesn't seem to mind. I roughed them up even more working on the rocking chair. I'm very, very proud of it. She sits there now, rocking my son in her arms, all tucked up in a ball of blankets and quilts, his fuzzy little head nestled against her chest.

Alexa yawns as I step back inside and quickly turn to close the door, more firewood tucked under my arms.

"We could get space heaters. Like normal people," she says, her voice thick from lack of sleep.

After I've fed the fire and cleaned up, I take him, bundled in blankets, and Alexa stands and stretches.

God, she's beautiful. We've decided to wait before having any more, but that hasn't cooled my desire for her. She started glowing when her belly grew and hasn't stopped. She still lights the room, pulls me along as she walks.

"I need a nap," she announces, yawning.

Aiden doesn't do much except nap, when he's not screaming. It's work, but it's good work. She's happy. My son is the only person in the world she looks at the way she does me, and somehow I'm not jealous.

Alexa climbs into the bed and pulls the covers up to her neck. Once she's asleep I sit next to her with my back up against the headboard and watch her. She's positively gorgeous when she sleeps.

She wakes up a split second before Aiden does. She always knows. Sitting up, she takes him in her arms then leans against me. I embrace my wife and child.

It's one of those phrases you hear but you never really think about what it means. Now I do. Happily ever after.

* * *

Abigail and I would like to thank you for buying *Riding Wood*. We hope you enjoyed this Sweet & Smutty Quickie, and we hope you'll leave us a review. We also have a special treat for those who sign up for our Sweet & Smutty List.

Sign up and get the first chapter of our upcoming novella, *Casting Couch*! Brace

yourselves, it's more instalove. SIGN UP HERE:
http://www.queensofromance.com/sweetandsmutty

ABOUT THE AUTHORS

Sweet & Smutty was born when Abigail Graham and Vanessa Waltz decided to team up to write short, steamy fun! Our novellas always end with a HEA. No ow/om drama. No cheating, *ever*.

We love hearing from fans! Drop us a line at sweetandsmutty@gmail.com any time!

60319685R00080

Made in the USA
Lexington, KY
03 February 2017